MARKED BY LOVE

A ZODIAC SHIFTERS BOOK

ROSALIE REDD

MARKED BY LOVE
A Zodiac Shifters Book

By

Rosalie Redd

For permissions contact: Rosalie@rosalieredd.com
Cover Design: Raven Blackburn

https://www.facebook.com/RavenbornCovers/

ISBN: 9781944419141
United States of America

CHAPTER 1

$\mathcal{D}$anae scooped up the tarot cards, one by one, her fingers trailing over the dark cotton tablecloth. She closed her eyes and took a deep breath, as much to stall as to calm her nerves. The cards were never wrong, although this time, she wished they were. Lavender, sweet and strong, filtered into her lungs, its calming effect easing the tension in her shoulders. At last, she opened her eyes and focused on her client.

The elderly woman tightened her grip around her tissue and wiped the cloth over her lips, the off-brand red lipstick a shade darker in the age lines around her mouth. Poor lady...rough times were ahead.

Since Danae had settled in the sleepy town of Brinnon, Washington a few months ago, she'd come to care for Amelia, one of the community's elder residents. On the edge of the Olympic Peninsula, the town, along with its neighbor, Quilcene, were a short ferry ride from neighboring Seattle. That brought a lot of tourist trade to Danae's palm and tarot card reading business, which worked in her favor, not only providing a steady source of income, but also a place for her to hide.

Danae settled her hand over the older woman's and gave her a gentle squeeze. "I'm afraid we're done for this week."

Through the thick lenses of her glasses, Amelia blinked. A few grey curls twirled over the frame. "Oh, yes, of course."

She wrapped her gnarled fingers around the worn wooden cane resting on the edge of the table. Her lips pursed, and her brows pulled together. With dogged determination, she pushed against the cane and stood. She wavered for a moment then a smile bloomed on her face as if she'd achieved a major victory.

Perhaps she had.

If the cards were any indication, victories would be hard to come by in her future.

Her movement stirred the air. Atop the antique desk, the bright red ember tip of incense flared to life, a line of ashes caught in the tail portion of the cat-shaped holder. Lavender, the key ingredient in Danae's homemade special paste was abundant from many farms in the area. It was a crucial component to hide her Panthera scent and keep the safe house hidden from her enemy, the Gossum.

With care not to seem too eager, Danae strode over to the older woman. She wanted to wrap her arms around her, help her to the door, but she'd get a whack with the cane if she did.

Been there, done that.

Instead, she walked next to her, providing moral support and a steady arm, if needed.

"Thank you, my dear. These weekly visits mean more to me than you know. I so appreciate your insights." She slipped a couple of twenty dollar bills into Danae's palm.

The money wasn't much, but it would help keep the safe house operating, at least for a while longer. She shoved the bills into her pants pocket and glanced around the old Victorian home. Two claw-foot chairs surrounded an old sofa, the wooden back marred with chips and nicks accumulated over the decades.

A threadbare rug sat under their clawed feet, as if the furniture had used the mat as a scratching post.

Her fingers twitched. Sometimes, her internal panther longed to do the same.

"Is Jeremy waiting for you?" Danae opened the old oak door. The squeak of the hinges pierced through the rain's constant drizzle.

Amelia removed her glasses and placed them in her sweater pocket. Creases formed around her eyes as she squinted. "Yes, my grandson is in the car. Here he comes."

The slam of a car door echoed off the house. A dark form headed up the walkway.

Amelia turned to face Danae. "Today is my birthday, March twenty-fifth."

"Yes, I remember. You're an Aries. Happy birthday." Danae's stomach twisted. She'd already wished the woman a happy birthday. Amelia's memory loss was another sign of the fate the cards had shown her.

"When is yours?" Her eyes, yellowed with age, glittered with curiosity.

I'll be 648 years old on my next birthday. A Panthera's life span could exceed well over three thousand years, but there was no way she'd tell Amelia that bit of info. Instead, Danae patted her on the arm. "August twentieth. I'm a Leo."

"Generous and warm-hearted. That suits you. I'm sure someday you'll find a good man, one that loves you dearly." The older woman chuckled and took a step forward.

Danae held her breath. That was so not going to happen.

Jeremy bounded up the two-step porch, umbrella in hand, and gripped his grandmother's arm. "I've got you."

With a swift flick of her wrist, she whacked her cane against his leg. "I'm perfectly fine."

"Ooof!" He rubbed the spot, and his gaze darted to Danae. He shrugged, his blue eyes twinkling.

Danae stifled a laugh. "Next week, Amelia?"

"Yes, see you then." The elderly lady gripped her grandson's arm and they headed toward the car. Rain slid down the umbrella and dripped off the pointy, metal tips. Cocooned beneath the material, Amelia huddled close to her grandson. The umbrella provided a bit of protection, but there were worse things to need refuge from than the rain.

Danae cringed. It was best for them that they weren't aware of the battle raging in the dark of night, the one that could enslave the entire human race.

Rain pinged against the large picture window. In the faint hues of early evening, a waterfall of liquid sunshine drained over the gutter. Her shoulders slumped.

Gary, the man who did minor repairs in exchange for some of her special incense, had fallen from a ladder last week at his home and broke his leg. He wasn't coming around anytime soon. She'd have to clean the gutters herself. Another thing to add to her already full to-do list.

Danae closed the door and leaned her forehead against the hard grain. The cool wood was a welcome balm against her skin.

A slow, familiar creak echoed from the top of the stairs. She stiffened. *Lamont.*

"Is the human female gone?" His deep, masculine voice sent a chill over her arms, raising the fine hair at her nape.

"Yes. It's safe to come down now." As she turned to face him, her claws elongated from her fingers, a natural defensive response. She clenched her jaw and forced herself to retract the pointed weapons.

With determined strides, he descended the staircase, his scuffed boots and dark jeans coming into view. His belt buckle reflected the light from the entryway, and her cat-like eyes constricted, blocking out the glare.

A dark shirt covered well-defined muscles in his abs and chest. As he continued his descent, his facial features became visible. Two days' worth of scruff covered his chin. His aquiline nose and high cheekbones were harsh, and his eyes, those haunted, yellow orbs, burned cold and hard.

A knot formed in her stomach. She headed for the kitchen, eager to put some distance between them. "I assume you're leaving. Would you like something to eat before you head out?"

"That would be generous." He stalked behind her, the floor shaking with every step.

She opened one of the cupboard doors, and the loose handle rattled against the wood, mirroring her shattered nerves. Her fingers curled around her favorite frying pan's handle. She yanked it from its resting spot and placed it on the burner.

"I have eggs and toast. Will that work?" Her voice wavered, and she mentally kicked herself for letting her uncertainty show.

He was just another rogue warrior here to rest in the safe house before continuing his fight for their goddess, Alora, against the Gossum.

Most warriors congregated in the underground Keep, the one hidden in the vast cave systems in the mountains of the Pacific Northwest. A few stray warriors fought the war for Earth's water on their own terms, searching for Gossum scouts. Yet, Lamont had made it a habit to stop by her safe house on a regular basis, his visits becoming more frequent.

The knot in her stomach tightened.

"That sounds lovely." He approached her from behind, and his scent of fire embers and coal overwhelmed her. After trailing his fingers through her hair, he brought a few strands to his lips. With much fanfare, he audibly inhaled. "I can't get enough of your lemony scent."

She pulled away from his grasp and tugged her dagger from her belt. Her pulse pounded loud in her ears. By touching his mouth to her hair, he'd left his pheromones, marking her in an intimate way.

With the tip of her blade, she pointed to the piece of paper tacked to the wall and strategically placed behind the chair set at the end of the kitchen table. "House rules state no touching the owner, among other things. Maybe you need to read them again."

He lowered his head in a mock bow, his gaze never leaving hers. "My apologies. No need."

She sheathed her knife and raised her chin. "Good. I expect you to abide by them. Now, about those eggs."

She followed his glance through the window into the darkening evening. The earlier rain was gone, and the moon's rays cast strange shadows over the landscape, turning treetops into sharp, pointy teeth. "Please, don't go to the trouble for me." His gaze narrowed, a tic pulsing in his jaw. "Duty calls me to the forest."

She released her pent-up breath. Despite her unease, she couldn't bear to see him, or any other warrior, go to battle on an empty stomach. "Here," she grabbed a couple of cookies from the plate nestled next to the cookbooks and condiments, "take these."

He stalked toward her. A slow, predatory smile revealed his pointed fangs. His fingers grazed over hers, sheltering the cookies in their combined grasps. "Thank you. Your kindness is...," his gaze dropped to her lips, then returned to her eyes, "exemplary."

Bitter and hot, bile rose in her throat, and she clamped down on the growl that started in her chest. With a quick tug, she pulled her hands away, leaving the cookies in his palm. "I thought I'd made myself clear. As a Panthera warrior, you are welcome in my safe house, but I expect you to abide by the rules. You've seen my weapon. I assume you know my reputation."

"Of course. A male or two mentioned your touchiness with that blade." He bit into one of the cookies, his fangs sinking into a chocolate chunk embedded in the soft dough. With a quick wink, he walked the short distance to the back door. He twisted the knob, and the bells hanging from the curtain rod jingled.

A moment later, he was gone.

She leaned against the counter, her ragged breaths coming hard and fast. Her trembling fingers curled into a tight fist. *Males can't be trusted.*

There was always a risk a rogue male would try to bite her, force her to mate to him. Over the years, she'd perfected her skill with her dagger, her throwing stars, and when all else failed, her claws. She traced the faded scar at the base of her neck. Once mated to a male she didn't love, she'd experienced betrayal firsthand.

Even to this day, the bitterness still stung. Thank the gods he was dead. A pang tugged at her chest. Despite her distrust, a part of her deep inside longed for something more.

She glanced out the window. *Sooner or later, I'll have to deal with Lamont.* Would he try to possess her? Her gut tightened.

In other circumstances she'd kill a male for threatening her, but they needed all the warriors they could get, and she wouldn't risk Alora's wrath nor weaken their position in the war.

Nervous energy raced through her veins. A run, that's what she needed, something to distract her from Lamont's disgusting leer. Before she could change her mind, she followed him into the dusky evening, but turned the opposite direction, putting as much distance between them as possible.

*a*ramond placed his palm against the cedar's rough bark. The tree's sweet scent infiltrated his senses and that was far better than the tart, astringent smell of his enemy. Yet, he itched to find a Gossum, take out his frustration on something other than himself. A twitch flitted across his eyelid, pulsing, tugging at the thin skin. He wiped his palm over his face, rubbing at the annoying tic.

In the darkening shadows of early evening, he focused his Panthera's shifter senses on the forest around him.

A stream bubbled over some rocks to his right, a mouse quivered under a bush to his left, an owl hooted. He flared his nostrils, breathing in the scents around him. On the air was the cedar, along with damp foliage, and the unmistakable bitter aroma of a Gossum—his enemy.

Distant, yet there.

He clenched and unclenched his fingers. For almost seven hundred years, he'd fought Gossum. Neither his kind nor the enemy belonged here. No, they played an elaborate game, a war. The prize—Earth's water and the fate of humankind. At least he worked on the right team, supporting his goddess Alora. Forced to avoid the killing rays of the sun, thanks to an error on Alora's part, night was their only time to battle the enemy, but winning this war was more important than ever now that he'd found his daughter. *Aramie.*

His breath caught in his throat. He brought his fist to his chest and rubbed at the pleasant ache. Her beautiful dark hair and brown eyes mirrored his own. Recently reunited with her, he couldn't bring himself to wander too far from the underground Keep.

Always on the move, he'd never had a territory of his own.

Yet, as an alpha male, he wouldn't bow down to another, not even his daughter's mate and Pride leader Demir. So, he did what he knew best, fought the battle on his terms, as a lone Panthera warrior.

He pushed away from the cedar and morphed into his panther, his clothes slipping beneath his fur. A long growl eased from his chest and echoed off the trees. His claws dug into the soft loam, his muscles burning with unspent energy.

He burst from his hiding spot, his paws flitting over the ground.

A sense of euphoria filled his chest, and he ran on, eager to find his enemy.

The astringent smell grew stronger, burning his nostrils. He slowed to a stop. His breath panted in and out of his lungs. He peered around a large boulder, searching for any sign of his enemy. Soft, muffled chuffs echoed through the surrounding trees. Branches in a nearby pine swayed to and fro.

The muscles in Aramond's back tensed, his hackles rising along his spine. On quiet feet, he closed the distance, stalking the creature like prey.

A crack rent the air.

One of the tree's branches fell, crashing into the underbrush. A shower of dew from the ground ferns flew into the air.

The grunts increased. A figure, hidden among the early shad-

9

ows, slipped from the tree. Once human, the creature still wore a pair of torn, ragged pants and the remnants of a shirt. His pasty bald head glowed in the dim light. A Gossum.

Aramond growled, alerting the creature to his location. What fun was it to take out the enemy without a fight?

The Gossum stood and focused his ink-black eyes on Aramond. A long, slow hiss eased from its lips, along with its long, pointed tongue. The end cracked like a whip, the barb glistening with poison.

Aramond prowled closer, his attention never leaving his enemy.

The Gossum placed his hand against a nearby pine tree. His fingernails extended, the tips digging into the bark. A few chunks rained down around his feet. He chuckled. "You can't win this war. We've received an influx of troops from the north. It's only a matter of time until you're all dead."

Aramond morphed into his human shape, his clothes reforming onto his body. He drew a throwing star from his pocket. The cool steel against his fingers was like an old friend, welcome and familiar. "The only death I see in the future is yours."

The Gossum moved away from the tree. He shot a glance over his shoulder. Perhaps assessing his escape route?

"Come now, don't tell me you're going to run. That's not sporting, but go ahead. I promise to make your death swift." Aramond smiled.

Branches in a nearby tree rustled. Another Gossum slithered to the ground, landing not far from his cohort. The newcomer wore a blue bandana around his throat. His claw-like fingers grazed over the material, snagging the end. "I like our odds better."

A shot of adrenaline poured into Aramond's veins, pinpointing his vision. "Do you now? Interesting, we'll just see how that plays out."

As a lone warrior, he'd fought multiple Gossum before and survived. Not that it mattered. There was no mate in his life to miss him. There was only one female he'd ever wanted and she'd mated to another male. His one regret...letting Danae slip through his fingers.

The first Gossum smirked. "Perhaps we can come to an agreement. A bargain, per se. Are you willing to hear me out?"

Aramond stepped closer, his boot squishing a mushroom poking through the soil. The more information he could obtain from his enemy, the better. "Tell me more."

A smile revealed the creature's serrated teeth. "Ah, got your attention did I? Good. I'm willing to extend an olive branch, so to speak. Come to our side, help us end this war. You will be well rewarded, of that, I promise."

"Really?" Aramond laced his voice with sarcasm.

"But of course. Enemies to friends, yes?" He raised the hairless skin over his eyes.

Aramond's fingers tightened around his weapon, the blade's edges slicing into his palm. The scent of his own blood filled the air. "You mistake me for something I'm not...a traitor."

Aramond launched his throwing star. The weapon whizzed through the air.

Loud chuffing sounds burst from the Gossum's throat. He ducked, but the throwing star hit its mark, embedding into the creature's dark orb. The Gossum slid to the ground, his torso and limbs disintegrating into a pile of black goo.

The male with the bandana took a step back, then bolted through the trees.

Coward...

Aramond strode with purpose to the dead Gossum. Wet sludge coated the ferns, forcing the fronds to lean over and bear the weight. A single point of his weapon poked through the muck, gleaming in the moon's light. He retrieved his throwing star, wiping his treasured possession against the moss along a nearby tree.

One down, one to go.

With a quick turn, he pursued his enemy deeper into the forest.

CHAPTER 3

*D*anae's paws scraped over the rock's edge, the jagged surface rough against the pads of her feet. Murhut Falls roared in the distance, the rumble of water sluicing over stone eerily similar to a growl. The scent of pine, fresh rain, and damp earth filled her senses.

No sign of Gossum.

She relaxed, the muscles in her back and shoulders easing.

Situated on the edge of a large ravine, her favorite pine tree beckoned. With practiced calm, she shifted into human form, her jeans, sweater, and tennis shoes reforming onto her body. She headed to her treasured spot and sat on the soft bed of pine needles. Several stuck to her palm, and she brushed them away.

After raising her arms above her head, she stretched, a pleasant ache ringing through her tired muscles. The run was what she'd needed, an opportunity to escape the house's confinement, her problems, and, most of all, Lamont.

Opening the safe house had seemed like a good idea at the time, a way to settle down and help out in the war. She blended in well enough with the local humans, but she hadn't anticipated the amount of repairs needed on the old place.

Without Gary's help, she wasn't sure she could keep the old Victorian.

A long sigh escaped her lips. Her gaze drifted upward. The galaxy lit up the night sky in a sparkling array of lights. Where was Orion, the hunter? She focused on the twinkling patterns, searching…searching…

There, on the horizon. Her chest expanded as familiar warmth filled her. Buried within the solar system of the third star on Orion's belt was her home, Lemuria. Someday, when either the war ended or she died, her spirit would return there.

Before she could stop herself, her gaze tracked along the path of Orion's belt until her focus landed on the Taurus constellation. The bull's most familiar feature, his face, was a series of stars in the shape of a 'V.' At one end, Aldebaran, the brightest member of the constellation formed the bull's bloodshot eye, glowing with an eerie red-orange hue.

He seemed to glare at Orion, menace dripping from his gaze.

A low growl eased from her throat, and her nails dug into the bed of pine needles. Taurus reminded her of Dradon when he was angry, for her dead mate's eyes had glowed a similar shade of red.

A slight wind kicked up, and a dry oak leaf skittered over the rocks at the edge of the ravine. Her nose twitched as she scented the breeze. The hair at the back of her nape rose.

Gossum.

She snarled.

With a quickness born of her species, she stood. Danae slid her hand into her sweater pocket and caressed the hilt of her dagger.

The crack of a large branch.

A feral cry.

The Earth shook with the beat of running footsteps.

Getting closer.

She turned toward the commotion. Traipsing through the

forest at a fast clip was her enemy. She couldn't mistake the bald head and pale skin. Once human, he'd had a life, probably on the streets of Seattle or Portland, one of the many homeless that sought refuge in the large cities. Her enemy preyed on the downtrodden, changing them from human men to Gossum with a single bite.

A part of her pitied the poor creature, but she'd kill him just the same given the chance.

He burst through the trees. At the sight of her, he stilled. His nostrils flared and his once human, dark orbs focused on her. A low, menacing hiss eased from his lips.

She pulled the dagger from her pocket.

His tongue whipped from his mouth, extending to its full six foot length. The barbed tip nearly hit her nose. Spittle landed on her cheek, wet and slimy.

Disgust roiled in her gut. She threw her dagger. It sailed through the air with a soft whoosh.

He jerked his head and the knife sailed past him, embedding into a pine tree with a loud thunk.

Crap. That was her only weapon, the rest still on her bedside table. She'd have to fight him in panther form.

A smile tugged at his lip, revealing his serrated teeth. He raised his hand, his blade-like claws glinting in the soft moonlight.

Movement flashed out of the corner of her eye. A male Panthera burst from the trees. Sleek and toned, his strong muscles flexed beneath his dark fur. He tackled the Gossum, taking him down. The pair rolled, end over end. Bits of rubble and pine needles scattered across the path in their wake.

The panther's snarl filled the air, along with his familiar scent.

She stilled. *Aramond.*

Even in his panther form, she recognized him. The dark sheen in his fur, the intensity in his eyes, the chip on the end of one fang. How was this possible? She hadn't seen him in over six hundred years.

I thought he was dead.

Something in her chest fluttered, but then bitterness filled her mouth.

Father lied to me.

She took a step forward looking for a way to help, but the pair battled too close together. Aramond bit the Gossum in the shoulder.

The creature screamed and raked its claws down Aramond's back.

Aramond lost his grip, his lips pulling tight over his fangs. The beast squirmed out of reach and took off, into the forest.

Aramond's hackles visibly rose, and a loud, furious snarl burst from him. He peered over his shoulder, his gaze narrowing on her. The fur on his back smoothed, the hackles disappearing.

She took a step toward him, curiosity pushing her forward. "Aramond?"

He shifted. In place of a large black panther, a tall male stood. He wore ragged blue jeans and a torn white T-shirt. Thick, dark hair covered his head and the shadow of a beard coated his strong jaw. Almond skin accentuated deep brown eyes that reflected the moon's rays. He was as she remembered—strong, stoic, beautiful.

Time seemed to slow. She held her breath.

"Danae…" His deep, soothing voice floated across the space between them.

"Where have you… Why did you…" The half-formed, painful questions tumbled from her mouth.

His brow furrowed over his arresting eyes. He stiffened, yet his nose twitched. His gaze scanned behind her into the forest before he flicked to the faded mark on her neck then met her eyes.

16

"Where is your mate...Dradon?" His voice turned harsh at the mention of her ex-mate's name.

She opened her mouth then closed it again, unwilling to risk herself with any male, even him. *Males can't be trusted.*

She took a step back.

Not far away, in the cover of the darkened forest, a hiss echoed—Gossum.

Aramond turned to face the threat.

She used his distraction to capitalize on the opportunity. After slipping into her panther form, she darted for the forest. Aramond brought back memories, recollections of a time long ago. Her fear of him, as much as of the Gossum, made her bolt. Eons ago, she'd trusted him, longed to bond with him.

Not anymore.

She couldn't allow him to find her. Maybe, if she was lucky, he wouldn't track her. Deep in her traitorous heart, a part of her prayed he would.

CHAPTER 4

*a*ramond approached the stream, his boots squishing into the soft mud along the bank. A cool breeze blew a few stray strands of hair across his cheek. He ground his teeth and forced the unruly locks behind his ear.

Closing his eyes, he breathed in deep, scenting the air, searching for any sign of Danae. A whiff of wet foliage, moss, and a nearby doe was all he discerned.

Danae's lemony scent was gone.

His jaw tightened. She must've crossed the water.

After their encounter at the top of the ravine, he'd wanted to chase after her then and there, but with the Gossum on the loose, he couldn't take the chance. The fight hadn't lasted long. He'd tracked and killed his enemy, but not without sustaining a few wounds in the process.

A drop of blood dripped from his fingertip, staining the green fern at his feet crimson. The lacerations on his back ached. Nausea churned in his gut. He knelt, scooped a handful of water into his palm, and splashed it onto his face. The cool droplets were a welcome relief to his heated skin.

Danae... Like so many times before, he ran his tongue over his chipped tooth. The familiar jagged edge, somewhat smooth from use and time, was a constant reminder of her. Chiseled into his bone as well as his soul, he couldn't deny the unstoppable love for her buried in his heart. To find her now was a torment like no other. His mind wandered to the last time he'd laid eyes on her and earned his damaged fang.

Aramond strode into the camp, his patrol done for the evening. The meeting place was full, many of the Pride coming to gather before retiring into their temporary, makeshift homes. A group of elders sat on an old fallen log next to the fire. Aramond approached close enough to feel the warmth on his cheeks, but kept a respectful distance.

One elderly male tugged the ragged blanket tighter around his shoulders and leaned forward. His gaunt face and weary eyes spoke of too many battles. Next to him, his female smiled and trailed her fingers over his palm. He patted her hand and intertwined his fingers with hers.

Aramond's chest expanded.

Someday, he planned to see a similar smile on Danae's face, once he'd convinced her to mate with him. After his mother kicked him out, he'd wandered for a few years, never feeling comfortable enough to join another Pride, not until he'd seen Danae on a run one day.

He'd followed her here and joined this Pride two months ago. It wasn't long before he'd fallen for her sweet smile and gentle laugh.

Yesterday was her fifteenth birthday. Now, she was eligible to mate. A tingling started in his fingers and raced up his arm. He couldn't wait to court her.

The leaves in a nearby oak tree rustled. Dradon strode into the clearing. At his side—Danae. Her shoulders were tense, and she kept her gaze on the ground. Twin bite marks, partially healed, marred the skin at the base of her neck.

Aramond's hackles rose. The urge to shift into his panther rippled over his skin. His fangs descended, his claws grew. He tensed, preparing to launch into his attack.

Traman, the Pride leader and Danae's father, brushed past Dradon.

Aramond stilled. As the newest and lowest ranking member of the Pride, he dare not attack now.

Traman would ostracize or kill him for his insolence.

"Good evening, everyone. I'd like to announce the bonding of my daughter to Dradon." Traman motioned them forward, toward the fire.

Gentle applause and a few uttered "congratulations" filled the air.

Danae's gaze rose and flitted over the crowd. When her attention landed on Aramond, she bit her lip. The fire's glow reflected the tears shining in her eyes.

Blood surged through Aramond's veins. Without conscious thought, he morphed into his panther, his pants and shirt disappearing beneath his fur. He snarled, his only warning, and launched himself at his rival.

"Aramond, don't!" Danae's words beat into his psyche, but he didn't slow.

He met Dradon mid-air, chest slamming into chest.

Dradon snaked a claw over his flank. The scent of his own blood filled Aramond's nostrils.

He bit Dradon on the shoulder. The cat screamed. Fur flew.

A heavy weight tackled Aramond to the ground. Dirt scraped his cheek. Low and menacing, a growl reverberated from his attacker. Aramond inhaled and Traman's unique scent infiltrated his senses.

The Pride leader clamped his jaw around Aramond's throat. His fangs pierced the tender flesh, just above the jugular vein. A thin trickle of blood dripped onto the soft loam. A warning... As much as Aramond didn't want to relent, he relaxed under the alpha's dominance. If he didn't, he'd die.

The heavy weight lifted from his back. Traman returned to human form and hoisted Aramond by the scruff. Aramond shifted as well, his clothes reforming onto his body. He faced the Pride leader.

"I've given you plenty of opportunity to fit into this Pride. No more." Still holding Aramond by the back of the neck, he shoved him away from the group, toward the forest. "Leave if you value your life."

Aramond glanced at Danae.

A single tear slid down her cheek. "Aramond, please, it's too late."

Traman's fist connected with Aramond's jaw. His head whipped to the side. Pain blossomed along his gum line. He scraped his tongue over his canine, the jagged edge tearing into his flesh. Coppery and bitter, the tang of blood filled his mouth. He spit the small piece of bone on the ground at Traman's feet and bared his fangs, one pointed, one now broken.

Growls emitted from the crowd. Several males stepped forward.

"Run. I'll give you a head start." Traman's words were low, menacing.

Aramond took one last look at Danae and fled into the forest. From that night forward, he was the alpha male in a Pride of one.

Aramond's fingers tightened around a fern growing along the water's edge. The frond shook in his grasp, bending in half from his pressure. He didn't remember grabbing the plant. Releasing his grip, he wiped the wetness on his pant leg and stood.

What had happened to Danae over the years? During his short time with her Pride, he'd taken every opportunity to be near her, falling for her faster than he'd thought possible. With a few stolen kisses from her soft, supple lips, she was forever imprinted in his memory.

He inhaled, replaying his encounter with Danae at the ravine. When he'd glanced at her neck, her mate's bite marks were almost imperceptible.

Dradon was dead, yet Aramond had smelled a male on her.

His pulse pounded at his temple. Where was her family? Other than Demir's Pride who lived in the underground Keep, there wasn't another one in the vicinity. He'd heard rumors from a rogue Panthera warrior about a safe house, hidden from the humans in plain sight, in a town not far away—Brinnon.

The hair at his nape rose as uneasiness tracked over his nerves. He'd avoided humans more than he'd avoided his own kind, and that was saying something.

Maybe, though, he could find out more information about

Danae and get some salve for his wound. Besides, unless he wanted an early death, he needed to find a place to hole up for the day, away from the sun's burning rays. He clamped his jaw.

Decision made, he slid from the water's edge and headed toward human civilization to find answers.

CHAPTER 5

*W*ith the potholder in her palm, Danae opened the oven door. The aroma of fresh baked cookies, a mixture of chocolate, dried cranberries, and sweet goodness filled the air. She wrapped her shaky fingers around the baking sheet and pulled the tray from the oven. The warmth from the open door chased away the chill, but even her favorite dessert couldn't calm her nerves.

Baking had always been her diversion when stress got the better of her. After a quick shower to wash off her run, she decided she needed the comforting activity more than ever.

She punched ninety seconds into the microwave's timer to allow the cookies a chance to cool before she removed them from the baking sheet. As she waited, she rubbed the bridge of her nose. *Aramond.* Her father's betrayal beat anew in her chest. Unable to stop the memory, that fatal night rushed through her mind, bringing back the pain full force.

Danae brushed the fine horse-hair bristles through her long tresses, catching on a knot only once. A few more minutes and Aramond would be here. Her chest lightened. She couldn't wait to see him. Today, she'd turned fifteen, old enough for the males to call upon her. With trembling fingers, she twisted her hair and pinned the thick strands into a tight bun.

Her father appeared in her doorway. A slow smile pulled at his lips. "You look lovely, my dear."

As she stood from her chair, the old wooden seat creaked. She ran across the dirt floor and leapt into his open arms. He held her for a long moment, his chin resting on her head. His soothing scent crept into her senses, warming her.

"My daughter. I love you." He released her and drew his finger down the side of her face. The skin around his eyes creased as he studied her. "Please remember, I have your best interests at heart, always."

"I know, Papa." She kissed him on the cheek.

"Dradon is here, waiting for you," he whispered.

Danae's pulse rose, her ears heating from the rush of blood. She glanced at her father. "I thought Aramond was the first to court me?"

"Aramond...was delayed. Dradon is here now. You shall see him." He gave her a wink and extended his hand, encouraging her to proceed down the hallway in front of him.

A heaviness settled over her shoulders. She so wanted to see Aramond instead, but she'd abide by her father's wishes. Aramond would get his chance. Her heart lightened a bit.

She tightened the cinch around her waist and wiped her sweaty palms over her thin woven dress. The material stuck to her sides, accenting her thin waist and full hips. She wished she had the same fullness in her breasts, but wishing wouldn't make it so, that's what her mother had always said. How Danae missed her.

With one final glance at her father, she proceeded down the hall. Dradon stood next to the small home's wooden door. A sliver of moonlight filtered through the nearby window, casting half his profile in stark relief, the other half in complete darkness. The juxtaposition sent a chill over her arms, the sweat on her palms now cold and clammy.

"Good evening, Dradon." Father nodded toward their guest. "Are you ready?"

Dradon bowed, his gaze never leaving her father's. "Yes, sir."

"Then proceed, you have my blessing."

Dradon glanced at her. His lips thinned, and his eyes changed color from a golden brown to a deep red.

Something fluttered in Danae's gut. "Wh...what—"

Before she could complete the thought, Dradon leapt toward her. He gripped her arms, propelling her backward with his strength until her bottom and shoulders connected with the wall. Air whooshed from her lungs. She struggled to breathe. White spots formed in her vision.

He grabbed her collar and yanked. The material ripped, the sound loud, terrifying. Cool air brushed against her exposed shoulder and chest. She pushed against him, but he was too strong. Her gaze tore to her father. "Papa!"

He stood still, unmoving, his emotions shuttered behind his stoic features.

Her heart raced.

A low, menacing growl burst from Dradon's throat. His fangs elongated.

A new wave of adrenaline surged through her. Before she could take another breath, he sank his teeth into the soft spot between her shoulder and neck. Pain rippled through her, as much from the penetration as the betrayal. She struggled still, even though the deed was done.

Dradon released her. Blood coated his mouth...hers. A dull throb beat at her throat. She touched the wound, two round puncture marks, wet with a mixture of his saliva and her blood. I'm bonded to him. *Her knees shook. Unable to bear her weight, she slid down the wall until her bottom hit the ground. Her attention tracked to her father. "Wh...why?"*

His lips thinned, his jaw tightening. "All females should be mated. It is the way of it."

She placed her head in her hands, but refused to let the tears flow. Her trust in males...shattered in a matter of moments.

The timer beeped, bringing her out of her reverie.

She gripped the spatula and with more force than necessary,

whisked the cookies from the pan. An ache ran up her arm from her tight fingers. Not only had her father orchestrated her forced bonding, he'd told her he'd killed Aramond for attacking her new mate and threatening him, the Pride alpha. The lie weaseled its way deep into her soul, adding another protective layer around her fragile heart.

With the last of the cookies resting on the rack, she tossed the spatula into the sink. It clanked against the stainless steel tub before coming to rest next to the mixing bowl. The muscles in her legs shook. She gripped the counter's edge to steady herself. A mewl of pure frustration eased from her lips.

"Father, if you were still alive, I'd spit in your eye." She spewed the words, spittle flying from her mouth.

She'd never get the chance. A few years ago, her father, Dradon, and almost everyone else in her Pride died at the hands of the Gossum. The few who'd survived hid in the woods. As individuals, they had a better chance to survive, lose themselves among the forest creatures. After wandering for a while, she'd ended up here, in Brinnon.

A knock on the back door made her jump. Goosebumps rose along her arm. *Stop, Danae. It's probably one of the locals.* She wiped her hands on the kitchen towel hanging over the refrigerator's handle and strode to the back entrance.

She tugged on the curtain and peered through the window. A shiver skated down her arms, tingling her skin along the way. *Aramond.*

His back was to her, his broad shoulders covered with a thin dark coat. Long, ragged gouges marred the surface along with something wet that glistened in the porch light's soft glow. He gazed along the path that led into the forest, his jaw tight.

Her heart stuttered at his strength and the determined set of his jaw.

Had he tracked her here? An odd mixture of trepidation and

anticipation brewed in her stomach, twisting and tightening into a knot.

She hesitated, her fingers hovering over the doorknob. *This encounter will change my life...one way or another.* The stray thought rambled through her mind, unbidden, unwanted.

She opened the door, and the bells hanging from the curtain rod jingled.

He turned to face her. His head jerked back and his lips, oh, those lustrous lips she remembered so well, parted. He blinked and tilted his head. "Danae?"

His brow furrowed. He took a step back. "I thought this was a safe house. Perhaps I've made a mistake. I won't bother you." He turned as if to leave.

Her heart skipped a beat. "Aramond, wait, please."

He stilled and peered over his shoulder. His deep brown eyes, filled with a torment she didn't know of, focused on her.

She glanced at the rips in his coat, the wetness more visible now that she was closer to him. Blood. A Gossum fight.

"This is a safe house...for warriors, like you." Her voice caught in her throat, and she had to swallow a few times before she could continue. "Please, come in. Let me help you with your injuries."

The proud warrior studied her for a moment longer. He gave a quick nod and approached her.

She stepped aside, holding the door open as he crossed the entrance. She'd let him into her home, but she'd be damned if she'd let him into her heart. So much time had passed since they'd last seen each other. He'd probably moved on, forgotten all about her.

She closed the door, and the bell tinkled its soft melody. His unique scent of earth and fresh rain permeated her senses, stirring a primal response in her she'd long forgotten. She stifled the purr building in her chest. "This way please."

As she stepped past him, his presence overwhelmed her, and she felt very small next to him, small and protected. A shiver rolled over her shoulders, from fear or excitement, she wasn't quite sure.

CHAPTER 6

*T*he scent of fresh baked cookies filtered across Aramond's senses, warm and welcoming. He stepped past Danae into a small dining area. The tick of a clock caught his attention. His gaze pulled to the wall and an image of a black and white cat, its eyes and tail moving in tandem with the staccato rhythm.

Nestled in one corner was a wooden table with four high back chairs. A glass vase, the color of the sea, sat on the smooth surface bursting with tulips in a brilliant shade of yellow. Why did she have those particular flowers on her table? A coincidence or something more?

Years ago, when they were both in the Pride, he'd brought her some of the same yellow flowers, the small gift letting her know he'd wanted to court her. The way her smile had brightened her features was burned in his memory.

Danae brushed past him. Her citrus scent mixed with the cookies' sweet aroma, blending into a unique, heady fragrance. *Sugar and spice and everything nice. Indeed.* The errant thought flitted through his mind, and he clamped down on the possessive growl that threatened to escape. The last thing he wanted was to scare her. At least there was no hint of a male. Perhaps he'd imagined the scent, or maybe that was wishful thinking.

She headed into the kitchen, giving him a good view of her backside. Tight jeans hugged her well-rounded buttocks and firm thighs.

His fingers twitched with the urge to grab one of her cheeks, give it a little squeeze, see her jump with surprise. But he did no such thing; he respected her far too much.

She gripped a handle on one of the old cabinet drawers next to the stove and tugged it open. The hinge screamed like a banshee. She bit her lip and glanced at him. Brown eyes, the color of rich, dark coffee, met his. It was as if she could see into his soul, knew everything that had happened to him since he'd been forced out of the Pride.

He swallowed the dry lump in his throat.

"Please, take off your coat, have a seat. I keep some of my medical supplies in here. Never know when a warrior will come in with some injuries." She blinked, pulling her gaze from him. With quick, efficient movements, she withdrew an assortment of gauzes, scissors, tapes, and antiseptics, placing them into a small tray.

He didn't move. Instead, he took the opportunity to study her. Silky dark hair flared around her shoulders, accentuating her fine cheekbones and the tip of her slender, upturned nose. Three gold studs pierced the edge of her ear, along with one alongside her nose and another over her eyebrow. The adornments were new, something she hadn't had the last time he'd seen her, well over six hundred years ago, but he liked the look.

The color accentuated the golden hue in her eyes.

She picked up the tray, her long slender fingers gripping the edge so hard the tips turned white. A quick glance at him and a frown marred her gorgeous features.

His chest tightened. He'd caused that reaction.

"Aramond, please, remove your coat…and your shirt, so I can tend to your injuries." Her words were tight, strained.

He did as she asked and slid the coat from his shoulders.

Her gaze flicked from his face to his chest as he gripped the edge of his T-shirt between his hands.

Primal and raw, his cat wanted to preen for her, and he forced himself to maintain his composure. With a quick tug, he ripped the material over his head. His skin screamed in protest, pain flickering over the open wounds, but it was worth it to see the look of appreciation in her eyes.

The shirt slipped to the floor. She motioned for him to sit.

He wrapped his fingers around the back of a chair and yanked. The feet scraped across the wood, echoing around the room. With a quick snap of his wrist, he flipped the chair around and straddled the seat, placing his arms along the chair's back.

A quick intake of breath.

He peered over his shoulder.

Her brow furrowed with a worried crease. A rawness coated the back of his throat. If only she would care for him, but he was as unworthy of her now as he was then.

She took clipped strides, rushing to place her assortment of tools on the table. The tray clanked against the wood. She stood so close he could reach out and touch her.

His fingers twitched again, and he curled them into a fist.

"These are much worse than I imagined. How are you…" She pursed her lips, and he had the sudden urge to kiss them, feel the plump flesh, warm and inviting against his.

His gaze flicked to the mark on her throat. Faded, the twin scars were barely visible. He couldn't stop the words as they tumbled from his mouth. "What happened to Dradon?"

She stiffened and her fingers tracked to the spot. "He's dead." She didn't elaborate, but grabbed several cotton balls and a plastic bottle filled with a white liquid.

"That much I can discern on my own. How did he die—" He inhaled.

Gently, she pressed the wet cotton ball against his back. The astringent stung, burning along the wounds.

"The medicine will work quickly. Along with your Lemurian blood, you'll be fine." Her fingers, deft and nimble, worked their magic, stroking the cotton over his skin in long strokes. Despite the pain, her touch burned like fire, lighting him up on a whole different level. His inner cat purred, and he couldn't stop the rumble in his chest.

She stilled, her hand on the small of his back. Before he could think about his actions, he flipped around in the chair, pulling her on top of him, her legs straddling his.

She squealed, and her hands landed on his chest.

The plastic bottle crashed against the floor, the fluid spilling from the spout.

He wrapped one arm around her waist. With his free hand, he brushed a few stray strands of hair away from her ear and toyed with the studs along her lobe. "Time away from you seems like an eternity, but I remember your touch like it was yesterday."

She inhaled, her breasts lifting, giving him a front and center view of her soft skin. Right before his eyes, two round nubs formed through the thin fabric of her shirt.

Blood pounded through his veins, heading south, and his pants tightened around the bulge at his crotch. He groaned.

Her eyes widened, and she squirmed, pressing against his erection. "Please, let me go. I have house rules. No touching."

"I'm sorry." The agony in those dark pools of brown bore into him. He rose to his feet, helping her to stand.

She took a step back, her hand covering her mouth.

He grabbed his shirt from the floor, along with the over-turned flask. He placed the plastic bottle on the table then shoved his arms through his shirt. With a quick tug, he pulled the material over his chest, glad for any sort of barrier.

She wasn't open to him. Did he really expect her to be? She'd just kick him out like every other female he'd ever known.

He grabbed his jacket from the back of the chair and headed for the door. "I should go. Thank you for assisting me."

"Aramond, wait." Her voice trembled.

His breath caught in his throat. He stilled and peered over his shoulder.

Her eyebrows knitted together. "Don't go, please. You asked about Dradon. He…died, along with almost everyone else in our Pride, including my father."

A cold chill ran down his arms. He turned to face her. "How? When?"

"Gossum. Three years ago. I escaped, along with a few others." She held out her hand toward the table. "I usually offer a meal to the warriors that seek medical attention here and a day's respite from the war. Please, stay for a while longer."

He held her gaze, a battle waging deep inside. If he stayed, he'd get hurt. If he left, he'd always wonder about her, about them. In the end, there really wasn't much choice. He'd stay long enough to find out more about her, make sure she was happy and safe then he'd leave before she kicked him out.

CHAPTER 7

*D*anae opened the cupboard, the hinge's squeak echoing off the kitchen walls. She cringed. "Sorry about that. One of these days, I'll get that fixed."

"I'd be happy to help." Aramond's rich baritone sent a shiver of delight over her skin.

She stole a quick glance at him. He stood near the end of the table, his attention focused on her house rules. His eyes tracked back and forth as he read.

Her heart skipped a beat, the reality of seeing him again toying with her emotions. She bit her lip and pulled two plates from the shelf. Thankful for yesterday's pot pie, she had plenty of leftovers to share. Grabbing a ladle, she scooped several heaping spoonfuls onto the dishes.

Before she could stop herself, her attention returned to him.

He'd moved on, now studying one of the posters on her wall, the one with the Taurus constellation. She had several throughout the home, each representing the twelve zodiac symbols. Why had he chosen this one to study? A chill crawled over her arms. Dradon had been a Taurus. Funny, in the time she'd known Aramond, she never knew his sign. Time to rectify that. Besides, a bit of small talk might ease some of the tension between them.

Gripping a plate in each hand, she headed for the table. The aroma of chicken, vegetables, and thyme filled the air. She placed the food on the tablecloth one plate on either side of the table.

He glanced at her, and a smile curled his lip. Her traitorous heart leapt into her throat. His smile had captured her from the start and still did. He was dangerous in an exciting, primal way. As much as she wanted to find out what had happened, she wasn't sure she could trust him, especially after he'd grabbed her. Not that she hadn't enjoyed his masculine scent, the strength of his arms, or his tender touch. Her earlobe tingled, the memory of his warm fingers caressing her in such an intimate way lighting up her nerves all over again.

She chided herself and sat down. "Dinner's ready."

"You're too kind. Thank you." He gripped the edge of the chair and slid into the seat. The wood creaked under his weight. His knee rubbed against hers, hard and firm, sending a brush of fire over her skin.

She inhaled. To cover her reaction, the first words that came to mind tumbled from her lips. "When's your birthday?"

His laugh was low, gentle. "You don't remember?"

Had he told her? She concentrated, her mind racing.

His chuckle came again, weaseling into her, stroking her insides. She had to fight the urge to touch his full, plump lips, see if they were as soft as she remembered.

"May first."

Her pulse rose. *Taurus.* Not what she'd expected or what she needed. She assessed his deep brown eyes. How possessive was he? Given the chance, would he bite her like Dradon had? Claim her without her permission? *No.* Yet, a twinge of uncertainty flitted over her nerves. Leo was supposed to tame Taurus, not the other way around.

He picked up his fork, holding it between his third finger and thumb, but he didn't eat. "After you."

She dug the tip of her fork into the pot pie, snagging a piece of chicken. Steam rose from the sauce and she blew on her food to cool it down.

He stiffened, the muscles in his arms tense.

She met his gaze. His dilated eyes were golden slits, the panther inside showing through. His gaze rose from her lips to her eyes, his voice low, husky. "Please, continue."

Warmth built in her chest, working its way toward the juncture between her legs. Not wanting him to sense her reaction to him, she squeezed her legs together.

His nostrils flared, and the embers in his eyes darkened to a deep, almost burgundy red. Just like Dradon…

Adrenaline poured through her veins, pooling in her gut. She placed her fingers over the dagger at her waist. He tracked her movements.

A soft chuckle eased from him. "Don't trust me? Can't say I blame you, but you have nothing to fear from me, Danae. I won't hurt you."

Her throat tightened. He said her name with such reverence, tingles of awareness raced up her arms. Unable to speak, she swallowed.

He bowed his head and returned his focus to his plate. "Thank you for your kindness and the meal."

They ate in silence for a few moments, the only sounds their forks clicking against the plates.

He wiped the napkin over his mouth, the material tugging on his bottom lip.

She couldn't stop herself from thinking about their last kiss, the one not long before Dradon had so viciously claimed her as his mate. Her chest constricted. She pushed back from the table and picked up his empty plate, along with her almost full one, and brought them to the kitchen counter. Her knees shook, a tremble rocking through her body.

The sound of his chair scraping against the floor eased across the room.

"Tell me something. Why are you here and not with Demir's Pride in the Keep?" His words had an edge to them.

She turned on the water and squirted a dab of soap onto the dishes. "You know about them?"

He rounded the end of the table and approached. Walking with the grace of his inner panther, the muscles in his arms and legs rippled as he moved. A part of her wanted to run her fingers over his taut muscles, feel the steel below the soft skin. She bit her lip and concentrated on the soapy dish in her palm.

He leaned against the counter, his broad, muscular hand flat against the worn countertop. Awareness of his closeness traveled over her arms, raising goosebumps.

"May I?" He pointed to the plate of cookies.

"Of course. Help yourself."

He gripped one between his thumb and forefinger and brought it to his lips. Opening his mouth, he bit into the soft cookie. At least with him, her hackles didn't rise at the sight. Instead, something warm stirred deep inside. She focused on the plate, giving some extra vigor to the scrubbing.

"Delicious." His smile turned serious, his lips thinning. "Demir's mate is Aramie. She's my daughter. I tracked her to this area."

Her hand jerked and the plate slipped from her grip, sliding under the water. *He has a daughter.* She searched his features. "Are...are you mated?"

Her pulse pounded, beating loud in her ears. She held her breath.

He shook his head.

The tenseness in her shoulders eased.

He ran his hand through his hair and let out a breath. "I didn't know I had a daughter. Chantre, Aramie's, mother kicked..." His jaw tightened before he continued. "She kicked me out before her scent changed, saying I was too much trouble. She didn't want a male hanging around. Had I known she was pregnant, I... Ah, *crap*." He stepped away, turning his back to her.

Long ago, his mother had kicked him out. He'd had no place else to go, that's why they'd accepted him into the Pride. His pain, evident in his stiff posture brought forth a wave of empathy.

A coil of tenderness wound around her chest, squeezing her rib cage. "So, you found her?"

He faced her, and his eyes glittered with admiration. "Yes, and I'm glad I did. She's wonderful, you'd like her."

Her heart fluttered. He cared for his daughter, loved her deeply. Maybe he still was the honorable male she'd once known. A part of her wanted to believe that were true. She shook her head. *No... I can't trust him. He could try to dominate me, like so many others.*

"Do you have any children?" His voice was tight.

"That never happened, thanks in part to the great scourge." Over five hundred years ago, the great scourge had wiped out many of their kind, leaving the remaining females infertile. In her case that was a blessing. She couldn't imagine what life would've been like for a child with Dradon as a father.

Aramond's shoulders relaxed. "So, you never answered my question. Why aren't you with Demir and his Pride, in the safety of the Keep?"

And that hit the nail on the head, didn't it? She dried her hands on the dish towel and tossed it onto the counter. *Stalling.* Yes, she was, but she struggled with what to tell him. "I...I..." She exhaled, and out of habit, her fingers tracked to the mark on her throat.

"I see." He took a step toward her. "You're afraid a male will force you to bond to him, just like Dradon. Is that it?"

"It's more than that." She didn't know Demir. As Pride leader, he would have dominance and control over her. What if he forced her to mate to a male, one she didn't know, one she didn't love? There was no way she'd go down that path again.

I'd rather take my chances on my own.

She studied Aramond for a moment.

"Then tell me, what is it?" His eyes never strayed from hers, his power and strength palpable between them. The urge to wrap her hands around his neck and bury herself in his arms to seek his comfort overwhelmed her senses. Her knees trembled.

She pushed away from the counter, brushed past him, and headed into the large living area. Through the picture window, the dark hands of night had relinquished their hold, the sky burning with the faint glow of dawn. "I have a room upstairs. It's the first one on the right. There's a washroom next door with plenty of towels."

"You don't need to do that on my account." His husky words burrowed deep into her chest, circling and searching around her heart.

She trailed her fingers over the scar at her neck, seeking strength. "You're welcome to stay. Providing a brief respite from the war to the rogue Panthera warriors is my way of helping out. I'll have a meal ready for you after sundown."

Before he could respond, she raced up the stairs. Her cheeks burned. She hated herself for running from him, but she couldn't face her past, couldn't face what he'd meant to her, what he still meant to her. She couldn't risk it, couldn't allow herself to fall for him again. If she couldn't trust her father, who could she trust?

CHAPTER 8

*A*ramond placed his boot on the last rung of the ladder and peered over the edge of Danae's roof. Sparkling in the moon's soft glow, a ratty shingle, one of many, curled at the edge. He shook his head. This place could use some attention.

Stored in the old shed at the back of the property, the ladder was an easy find. Aramond pressed his boot tighter against the step, using the edge for extra balance. Not that he needed it. If he fell, he'd land on his feet, thanks to his natural panther instincts.

He slipped his hand into the gutter. His fingers pressed into a pile of leaves and pine needles, still wet from the day's rain. He gripped a handful of moist debris and tossed it into the bucket sitting on the ladder's small shelf. The wet leaves sloshed against the bucket's edge, a few slipping to the ground.

He'd wanted to help out in some way, thank Danae for her kindness—for letting him stay. She hadn't kicked him out, not even after he'd pushed her about her obvious fear over bonding to a male. Her refusal to answer spoke volumes.

His teeth ached from his clamped jaw.

A few drops of water dripped into the puddle under the ladder. The rhythmic splashes had alerted him to the problem.

When he'd spotted the pool of water and the bits of leaves protruding from the gutter, he hadn't hesitated.

The need to provide for Danae, protect her, do what he could in any small way to make her happy, had set him in motion.

His chest expanded as he worked. If he were honest, he'd admit that he did this to prolong his time with her, but he couldn't afford to get too attached. Something would go wrong, and sooner or later, she'd kick him out.

The front door opened and Danae stepped outside. She wore jeans and a pretty, sheer blouse, the fabric showcasing all her glorious curves. Her dark hair hung loose around her shoulders, accentuating the golden brown in her eyes, but the resolve burning in her gaze really caught his attention.

His pulse picked up.

"What are you doing?" Her soft voice floated along the breeze.

He descended the ladder. "Fixing your gutter. Seems to have overflowed a bit."

She took a step forward, her small black flats not something he expected with the outfit, but it matched her personality—no nonsense and down to earth. Her brows rose above those beautiful baby browns. "Thank you, but you didn't have to do that. I have a guy…"

The muscles in his legs tensed and he stopped mid stride. *Guy? What guy?*

His stomach hardened and his breaths came faster, coarser.

She must've noticed a change in his demeanor for she blinked. "Umm…I had a human male from the town come once a week to do minor repairs around the place, but he fell," her eyes darted to the ladder, "off a ladder and broke his leg. Thank you. That…this is very helpful."

With a quick intake of breath, she bit her lip. The possessive urge to kiss her until she remembered only him—wanted only him—burned in his gut.

Instead, he gave her his best smile, encouraging her. "You're welcome. It was my pleasure. Is there anything else I can do?"

There were several repairs needed around the place—shingles for a few bare spots on the roof, wood cut for the fireplace, a good mow, just to name a few. He'd do them all if she asked.

Her brows pulled together. "I'm almost out of wood for the fireplace. You sure you don't mind?"

His chest expanded. "Not at all. It would be my pleasure, a way to repay you for your hospitality."

The edge of her lip curled into an adorable smile, the one he remembered from so long ago. "There's bacon, eggs, and toast inside. Please, come in, share the food with me. I don't want them to get cold."

He couldn't resist her, not then, not now. The need to touch her raced along his nerves, lighting up the sensitive pads in his fingers, but he wouldn't give in to his impulse. Her house rules were clear—no touching. Seems he'd already broken that rule when he'd pulled her onto his lap. He wouldn't make that mistake again.

She held open the door. He followed her inside.

❧

The crunch of tires against the gravel driveway and the hum of a car's engine receded into the night. Aramond hefted the axe over his head and brought it down on the wood. A loud crack rent the air and the firewood split into two pieces. He picked them up and added them to the stack. The muscles in his back and arms ached from the workout.

He smiled. It was almost better than taking down a Gossum. Almost.

After their meal, Danae had mentioned she had a few clients scheduled to come over. To run this place, she gave palm and tarot card readings to the human tourists and locals that lived in the area.

An ache from his clenched teeth radiated up the side of his face. The idea of interacting with the humans didn't sit well with him. At least in human form, the Panthera looked like an ordinary human and she seemed to blend in just fine.

With more force than necessary, he brought the blade down again and split another piece of wood in two. Situated in the backyard next to the shed, the woodpile was almost full. He glanced at the house. A shadow passed over the kitchen window's curtains. *Danae.*

Restlessness twisted in his gut. He'd done what he could around the place for one evening. There was no excuse for him to stay. He needed to get on with his job, find and eradicate Gossum. As much as he wanted to remain here, he couldn't. Besides, she'd end up kicking him out in the end, might as well get it over with now.

Something moved in the shadows on the edge of the forest. He stilled, releasing his grip on the axe's handle. It slid to the ground and landed in the soft grass with barely a sound. He inhaled, sniffing the air. The scent of fire embers and coals filled his nose—another male Panthera. Aramond's entire body stiffened, his muscles rigid with tension.

The male walked up the steps, oblivious to Aramond. He had on a dark jacket, his black hair spilling over the collar. A burning started in Aramond's chest, heat radiating up his neck and into his face.

Was this male a rival or just another warrior looking for a meal and a place to stay for the day? Aramond's attention didn't waver.

The male knocked on the wooden doorframe, the sound echoing off the trees at the edge of the property. Within moments, Danae opened the door.

Aramond took a step forward, then another. Would she greet him?

Lines formed around her eyes, but she smiled. "Lamont, I didn't expect to see you again so soon."

So, she knew him.

Still, Aramond didn't relax. He continued his slow prowl.

Lamont closed the distance, invading Danae's personal space. "May I come in?"

She took a step back. "Of course. I have some leftovers if you're hungry."

With a quick move, the male shoved Danae through the doorway. A loud, feral cry burst from his lips.

Danae! Adrenaline propelled Aramond forward. He morphed into his panther and lunged across the grass. *Alora, my goddess, help me get there in time.*

CHAPTER 9

*L*amont gripped Danae's arms, forcing her backward. Her heel connected with the baseboard. Pain shot up her leg.

He shoved her against the wall, his knee between her legs, his hands wrapped around her forearms, pinning her in place. The zodiac pictures on the wall rattled.

Her pulse spiked. The need to defend herself skimmed over her nerves. She slammed her forehead against his nose.

"Argh!" His grip loosened.

Forcing down the fear that wrapped around her muscles, she reached for her dagger. Her fingers tightened around the familiar hilt.

He pressed his chest into her, squishing her hand between them. A low growl rumbled in his chest. His eyes turned into yellow slits, deepening to a scarlet glow. The stark white of his fangs gleamed in the light.

She squirmed, kicking and bucking against him. "Let me go!"

"You *will* belong to me." His hot breath reeked of something bad, rotten.

No! She wouldn't be a mated female again. Fighting harder, she kicked, squirmed, and bared her fangs, doing anything to stop him.

A loud crash. Broken glass tinkled on the parquet floor.

A blur of something dark flitted across her vision too fast for her to identify.

In the next instant, Lamont's grip on her broke and he tumbled backward. She was free. Adrenaline surged through her veins.

A black panther pinned Lamont to the floor. *Aramond.*

She inhaled and pulled her dagger from its sheath.

Lamont morphed into his cat, nearly matching Aramond in size. A deep, menacing growl erupted into the room. The larger panther dug his claws into Lamont's flank. Blood pooled along the long deep scratch. Lamont bit Aramond in the shoulder. Claws, teeth, and tufts of fur melded into one as they fought.

She took a step forward, dagger in hand. Her chest tightened. The males were too quick, she couldn't risk hitting Aramond.

They battled, tooth and nail, rolling into the kitchen. Aramond crashed against the table leg. The wood splintered, sending the table careening to the ground. A vase holding flowers tumbled off. Glass shattered into a hundred shards and skittered across the floor. Beautiful yellow tulip petals lay like dying soldiers on a battlefield, scarred and broken.

Aramond snarled, the sound reverberating off the walls. He scraped his claws down Lamont's face, gouging his nose. Blood splattered across the floor. Lamont yelped and jumped away. His gaze flicked to her, his red eyes penetrating into her soul.

She placed the blade between her thumb and forefinger and raised it over her shoulder, intent on burying it in one of those crimson orbs.

Aramond stood, bits of glass and wood stuck to his dark, thick coat. He moved forward, tracking the other male.

She pressed her fingers tighter against the dagger's blade. "Get out, Lamont."

He took a step back, then another before bolting through the broken door. Aramond chased after him, bloody footprints left in his wake.

"Aramond! Wait!" With trembling fingers, she slid the blade back into its sheath and followed him.

She didn't have to travel far.

He stood on the porch step in his human form, glaring after Lamont. His broad shoulders heaved, his breath coming hard and fast. "Stay away from her. If you come back here, you'll have to deal with me."

Her heart fluttered as that part of her she'd closed off slowly awakened. His protective nature was so like the young male she remembered. She placed her hand against his back, leaning close. His warmth was like a balm to her shattered nerves.

Lamont stood in the yard, the muscles in his shoulders and hindquarters tense. He morphed into his human form, his dark clothes reforming over his body. A large scratch ran over the bridge of his nose. Blood welled in the cut, shiny in the moonlight. He curled his lip. "Challenge accepted, another time."

He trotted into the forest, disappearing from sight.

Aramond turned to face her. He reached out to touch her, but his hand stopped in mid-air. One eyelid twitched. His gaze traveled over her features then darted to her neck. He let out a huge breath and bowed his head. "Are you all right?"

She trembled, the reality of her close call catching up with her. The need to touch him, have his comforting arms around her burned inside. She trailed her finger down his arm. "Y...yes, I'm fine."

His eyes darted back and forth as he studied her. "I'd like to hold you, if that's okay."

She gave a quick nod.

He tugged her close, wrapping his strong arms around her. She melted under his tenderness and settled her head against his chest. His heart, strong and rhythmic, beat loudly beneath her ear. She breathed in his unique scent and it worked its way inside, calming her.

He stroked his fingers through her hair, massaging her scalp. "Hey, hey. He's gone now."

She wanted to stay this way, cuddled in his arms, protected, cared for…loved. A tension she didn't want, one borne of years under a male's firm control, darted over her shoulders.

He stilled. Pulling back, he cradled her head in his palm, his gaze searching hers. "What is it? What's wrong?"

The tender, caring sparkle in his brown eyes just about broke her, but Dradon had been kind and tentative up until the moment he'd bit her. Who's to say Aramond wouldn't do the same?

She shook her head. "It's nothing. You're hurt." Blood had darkened a spot on his shirt at the shoulder. "Let me get my medical kit."

He gripped her hand, stopping her. "I'm fine. It's just a minor scratch. I'll heal in no time."

She peered into his eyes, this strong, proud warrior. Her throat tightened, holding back any further words, so she nodded her acquiescence.

He exhaled and glanced at the carnage around him. "I'm sorry about the door. There's some plywood in the shed. I'll put that up until you can get a new one."

"Thank you," she whispered. This male had saved her from a forced mating. How could she think he'd be anything other than honorable? Her tormented past brought forth her insecurities and as much as she wanted to, she couldn't bring herself to trust him.

He squeezed her hand. "Let me get the plywood. I'll be right back."

He took off through the grass before she had time to stop him. Her shoulders slumped. Glass shards, broken wood, and tulip petals were spread over the entryway and kitchen floor. The flowers were a reminder of her past, a time when she'd longed to be with Aramond, had wanted to be his mate more than anything.

Now, though, the flowers were like her life—broken, discarded, shattered—and why she protected her heart.

After a quick tug on the closet door, she gripped her broom in one hand and the dustpan in the other. Time to start on the mess. If only she could clear away the wreckage in her damaged soul so easily.

CHAPTER 10

*A*ramond pounded the last of the nails into the plywood. He brushed his forearm over his brow, wiping away a bead of sweat. The ache in his shoulder burned, the scratches a bit deeper than he'd thought. His rage bubbled to the surface, hot and raw, and he curled his fingers around the hammer's handle, claws biting into the rough wood. That male, Lamont, had almost bitten Danae.

A rough growl burst from his throat.

What would he have done if she'd slipped through his fingers, claimed by another male? After all these years, seeing her again brought back feelings he'd thought long dead. He cared for her, more than he should, and she'd only end up kicking him out.

That's how it always ended. Not that he'd tried to claim a female before. There was only one he'd ever wanted—Danae.

"Aramond?" The soft lilt of her voice trickled through his thoughts. Like the tune of a favorite song, the melody wrapped around his heart, squeezing it tight.

She peered around the short wall separating the entryway from the kitchen. A smile tugged at her lips, and when it bloomed on her face, happiness glinted in her eyes. "Would you help me with the table?"

"Of course." Damn, he'd help her with anything she asked.

He tracked the short distance to the kitchen. Missing a leg, the table leaned to one side. A pile of books, stacked one on top of another, stood in place of the absent post. He scanned the titles —*One Lonely Cowboy, Highlander's Romp, My Forever Lover*, among others.

He chuckled. "Romance novels?"

She placed her hands on her hips, but that smile, the one he couldn't resist threatened to form. "You should try one sometime. Besides, I did the best I could with what I had."

"I guess that will do for now, until I can fix it for you." He stilled. What was he thinking? He couldn't stay here. His job was to hunt Gossum.

Fortunately, she ignored his comment, letting him off the hook. "Please, help me with the—"

"I got it." He lifted the end of the heavy table and placed it on top of the books. The old paperbacks sagged, but held the weight.

"Thank you." She wrapped her arms around her waist, holding herself in a tight grip.

A lump formed in his gut. She'd gone from happy to sullen in a matter of moments. "Danae?"

Vulnerability reflected in the depths of her soft brown eyes, and they glistened with unshed tears.

He strode to her, and then wrapped her in his embrace.

Accepting the comfort he offered, she leaned into him. A shudder wracked her small body. His jaw tightened, and he swore he'd beat that cat to a pulp if he ever saw him again. He stroked her hair, talking to her, a string of nonsensical words falling from his lips—you're okay…he's gone…shhh… Her trembling slowed. Wet from her tears, his shirt clung to his chest.

She pulled away, searching his features, and her red-rimmed eyes flitted back and forth. Her lip quivered. His gaze fixated on her mouth, and he wanted to kiss her, find out if her lips were as soft as he remembered. Instead, he gave her space, something she seemed to need so desperately.

"I've fought off many a male over the past few years, but if you hadn't..." Her fingers tracked to the faded scar on her neck. "I'd be a mated female." Her tone turned harsh.

She pushed away from him. Her eyes burned with a determination he hadn't seen before. "I can't...I won't go there, not again, not ever."

His gut tightened. As much as he wanted to claim her himself, he would never force her. He hadn't when they were youths and he wouldn't now. Lowering his voice, he spoke quietly. "You don't have to."

She studied him for a moment then turned toward the living room. Her quick footfalls echoed on the wooden floor. He followed, willing to offer her any emotional support she needed.

Arms crossed, she stood next to the giant picture window. The faint light of dawn brightened the sky. On the antique desk next to the worn davenport the tip of an incense glowed, a trail of ash caught in the holder—the long tail of a black cat. Fresh lavender aroma filled the air.

Danae held her chin up, and her mouth drew into a thin line. She wore her tenacity and determination like a shield around her heart. If only he could break through that barrier. He wouldn't force her to do anything, but he vowed to put a dent in that armor, for her own good.

"The sun will be up soon. Will you stay here with me?"

"Of course I will." He couldn't leave now if he'd wanted to. Walking up behind her, he ran his hands down her arms, rubbing them. "Tell me. What happened that night, when you became Dradon's mate?"

He focused on her features, trying to read her thoughts.

She stared through the window at the last remnants of the night sky. A handful of remaining stars twinkled, fighting to stay visible among the brightening light. Only a few more minutes before sunrise.

Her brow furrowed. A soft sigh eased from her lips. She relaxed into him, the tension in her shoulders easing. Her hair teased his chin, her lemony scent mixing with the lavender and burning into his senses. "I came downstairs, wearing a pretty new dress. I was so happy, expecting to see you."

He stopped his caresses, resting his fingers against her elbow. She'd wanted to see him. He swallowed and continued stroking her arm.

"Instead, Dradon waited for me. My father asked him if he was ready. I remember being confused at his question." A short, stifled laugh burst from her mouth. "At fifteen, I thought I'd had a choice. How naive. Dradon attacked me. I screamed for Father. He stood there, watching."

Aramond's jaw tightened to the point of pain. "I'm sorry I wasn't there for you."

She turned to face him, placing her hands on his biceps. The skin on skin contact lit up his nerves. He wrapped his arm around her waist, holding her close. Through moist eyes, she studied him. " 'Females should be mated. It is the way of it.' Those were my father's exact words."

Her pain found a way into his chest, heaviness settling into his heart.

He trailed his fingers over her forehead, moving away a few stray strands of hair. The betrayal...no wonder she didn't trust males. He wanted to reach through time, pound his fist into her father's face.

"Before, when you asked me about Demir and why I wasn't with his Pride, I didn't tell you the real reason I don't want to go to the Keep." Her lip trembled.

He cupped her cheek in his palm and stroked his thumb over the tender flesh. "You don't have to."

"But, I want to." Her words were soft, quiet.

He held his breath, wanting her to trust him, believe in him.

"Demir...he'll force me to mate..." A tear slid over her lashes, landing on her cheek.

He wiped it away with the back of his finger. That she would share her fear endeared her to him, and his chest ached for her. "This makes more sense to me now, why you're here. I don't know Demir well, but my instincts tell me he wouldn't force a male on you."

She nodded and a relieved breath escaped on a short laugh.

He tugged her tighter against him, cradling her, wanting her to see how much he cared for her. "You deserve so much better. I would never...will never...force you, Danae, not ever."

She brushed her fingers over his shoulders and around the back of his neck. His skin tingled at the contact. She drew her gaze to meet his. In the depths of her dark eyes was a glimmer of trust. Hyper-aware of her scent and her touch, his pulse raced. After all these years, he still loved her. The truth hit him in the chest, hard and fast. His ribs ached so much, he couldn't breathe.

Her tongue darted from her mouth, moistening her plump, inviting lips.

"Kiss me." Her whispered words brushed over him, and he couldn't deny her request.

Cradling her head in his palm, he lifted her chin, preparing her for his kiss. Her breath came fast, her chest rising and falling in anticipation. With deliberate slowness, he lowered his lips until they brushed against hers, soft and light. A tingle of energy rippled between them, hot and electric. She trembled in his arms and a soft whimper eased from her throat.

Her soft declaration of need fueled his desire, and a rush of blood pooled in his groin. He wanted her, more than he'd thought possible. Bringing his lips to hers in a bruising kiss, he poured all the pent-up love for her he'd harbored over the years.

Hard and fast, her nails dug into his scalp with a possessiveness he hadn't anticipated.

Tightening his grip around her waist, he pressed his hard, straining erection against her abdomen. Even through the material, the warmth and softness of her skin was irresistible.

With tenderness, he licked the sensitive skin along the seam of her bottom lip. She opened to him on a gasp. He took advantage, exploring her, bringing back memories of the few stolen kisses he'd obtained so long ago. Those were the kisses of two youths. This…this was something more, deeper, a passion he'd wanted for so long. *Only Danae.*

He pulled away to give them a chance to breathe. Their combined panting filled the space between them. Cradling her chin in his palm, he placed his forehead against hers. "Danae, what you do to me."

She smiled, and a soft giggle eased from her lips.

The sun's rays crested over the tree tops, bright and beautiful. He released her and stared at the sight. Only once in his life had he seen the sun. "Look."

She followed his gaze, her eyes squinting from the glare. "It's gorgeous, isn't it? We can't stay here. The sunshine will poke through the window soon. I've watched it travel over the carpet many a day."

Unwilling to let her go, he held her close for a moment longer. She stroked her fingers down his arm, her nails lightly scraping over his skin. Placing her palm in his, she stepped away and gave him a gentle tug. "Come with me."

Ah, hell. Every fiber of his being screamed that she was the one, his true mate. He wanted more from her than one day, but he wouldn't force her to bond to him. Instead, he'd show her what she meant to him and pray she didn't kick him out.

CHAPTER 11

*D*anae's heartbeat pulsed in her throat, a mixture of anticipation, excitement, and nervousness. Dradon was the only male she'd ever been intimate with. Not that she could call what they had intimate.

A niggle of fear tingled along her nerves, but her desire, the pure need for Aramond rushing through her veins outweighed the unease. He'd promised he wouldn't bite her and she believed him. He was honorable.

That hadn't changed over the years.

She tugged on Aramond's hand and led him up the stairs. As her foot settled onto the top step, the familiar groan creaked from the wood.

"Good thing you don't have a house full of guests." His low voice held a hint of amusement.

Her stomach fluttered, and she stifled a laugh. "I think the squeak is the least of the noise they'd hear today."

A purr rumbled from his chest. "That's a challenge I'll accept."

Danae gripped her fingers around her bedroom doorknob and twisted. The latch clicked. A soft push and the door swung open. Tightening her grip on his hand, she strode into her room.

She drew her dagger from her belt and tossed it onto the bedside table. It clattered against the lamp base before settling next to her clock.

Aramond wrapped his strong arms around her waist, drawing her back against his front. His erection, hard, firm, and long pulsed against her bottom.

Her body responded, sending a rush of wetness to her core. She shivered with delight, goosebumps forming on her arms.

With a quick turn, he flipped her around to face him. Warm and heady, his masculine scent of earth and fresh rain filtered into her senses, heightening a release of her own pheromones. The distinct aroma of lemons filled the air. Heat rose to her cheeks, and she bit her lip.

He chuckled, the low rumble reverberating in his chest. Even through her clothes, the sound tickled her nipples pressed against his firm abs. She laced her hands in his hair, gripping a few strands between her fingers. Danae growled, a rough and demanding tone.

"You drive me insane," he hissed.

Before she could respond, Aramond pulled her to him, his lips claiming hers. The intensity in his kiss sent her into a spiral of need so raw, she couldn't stop herself. She pressed against him, meeting his tongue stroke for stroke. Unwilling to let him go for even a moment, she tugged at the edge of his shirt. He didn't seem to need any further encouragement.

Aramond broke their kiss long enough to strip the white T-shirt from his chest. The briefest hint of daylight filtered under the heavy curtains covering the windows, but it was enough for her catlike vision to pick out his broad and rippled chest. His unblemished skin, healed from his fight, took her breath away. She ran her hands over him, enjoying the strength beneath the soft skin.

A purr of pure admiration rumbled in her chest.

He fumbled with the buttons on her shirt, but his large fingers were too big to handle the small fasteners. His brow furrowed as he concentrated, frustration etched in his dark eyes.

Danae couldn't bear to see him look that way, so she helped him, as eager as him to rid herself of the confining garment. She wiggled out of the shirt, and his eyes widened at her blue and yellow floral bra.

He toyed with the straps and his finger grazed along the edge of the cup, the rough calluses on his fingers teasing her skin. Her nipples peaked, her anticipation growing. He didn't make her wait long. With a glimmer of pure reverence in his eyes, he trailed one finger under her cup and over her taut nub. A moan eased from her throat, and she gripped his biceps. The muscles tightened under her palms, hard and firm.

"I like your choice of undergarments. Floral is nice, but it has to go." His teasing words were rough, deep.

A part of her melted for him, right then and there, breaking through a piece of her wall. He reached behind her and unhooked her bra. Tenderly, he slid the straps down her arms until the garment slipped to the floor. He stepped back and her chest ached at the loss of contact.

A breeze from the open window fluttered the curtains, the sound gentle like a moth's wings, matching the tremble in her heart.

With deliberate intent, he perused her, studying her with his full attention. An appreciative smile curled his lip. "Danae...you are so beautiful."

Her heart broke open at his declaration, and she ran her finger over his bicep and down his arm. "I can't tell you how many times I..." ...*fantasized about you.* She couldn't bring herself to say the last few words. Her jaw tightened. He couldn't love her, not really, and she couldn't give herself to him completely.

"Hey, hey. It's okay." Aramond pulled her into his arms and kissed her.

His tenderness, his strength, and his compassion engulfed her, as he comforted her in his embrace. He broke the kiss and trailed his lips down her face and over her ear piercings, tugging each one into his mouth then lowered himself on one knee, avoiding her neck and her collarbone, aware of her sensitivity there. With a gentleness she'd never known, he pressed his lips on her chest, right over her heart. Tears formed in her eyes, and she dug her hands into his hair.

He cupped her breast in his palm and flicked her nipple with his callused thumb. The tip peaked for him, hardening even more, and a shot of desire fled from her nipple to her core as if connected on an invisible string. He trailed a few kisses over her breast before taking the taut globe into his mouth. Danae bucked against him at the contact, but he refused to let her go, his arms wrapped around her waist.

A half-chuckle, half-purr erupted in his throat, sending another shock wave through her body. She responded to him as if he owned her, and a part of her screamed in protest, while another part relished in the thought. Her brain spun, heady from his onslaught and her confused emotions.

Aramond tugged at her jeans, and she didn't need any further encouragement. She wrenched at the zipper, and between the two of them, they were off in a matter of moments, along with her flats and panties. Wanting him as naked as her, she fumbled with his belt buckle.

He gripped her hand, stopping her. Danae met his gaze. "Not yet. I want to enjoy you first."

The look of pure adoration and deference in his brown eyes melted her on the spot. She wouldn't refuse him.

"Okay." Her breathless word squeaked from her lips.

He worshipped her hips and thighs with his soft touch. Giving a gentle nudge, he encouraged her backward until her bottom rubbed against the edge of the bed. The cool, soft comforter was a welcome balm against her heated skin. With a quick move, he gripped her thigh and placed one leg over his shoulder.

Exposed, cool air connected with her swollen folds, the breeze stimulating and erotic. A rush of moisture coated her sheath.

His nostrils flared, and a flash of red sparked through his eyes. Instead of bitterness and control—desire, admiration, and love reflected in their depths.

Tenderness and need twisted in her gut, but she didn't get time to dwell on it for his lips pressed against her mound. Tendrils of electricity shot to her clit, hardening it.

With a slow, languid stroke of his tongue, he licked her soft folds.

Sparks of light flitted over her vision. Holy hell, the things he could do with his tongue. Danae squirmed under his onslaught, her hands tightening over the bedspread, bunching the material between her fingers.

Aramond teased her, licking and stroking, but when he circled his thumb over her nub, that was her undoing. On her next breath she screamed, the orgasm taking her out on a wave of want and need she'd never experienced before. The vexing male didn't stop until he'd tormented every last shudder from her. She relaxed and reclined on the bedspread. He pressed his cheek against her thigh and blew on her clit. She shivered, sated and happy. "Aramond, it's your turn."

CHAPTER 12

*D*anae's sweet voice wound around Aramond's heart. *It's your turn.* His balls tightened and his erection pulsed painful and hard against his jeans. *Craya,* she had him in the palm of her hand. Crook her finger and he'd do whatever she asked. She'd always had that effect on him, and he was lost to her now.

She spread out on the bed, arching her back, teasing him with her perky breasts and her well-rounded hips. Danae was a goddess. *No offense, Alora.*

Danae patted the bed, a wicked smile gracing her lips.

He stood and gripped his belt buckle. Her attention focused on him, and her smile wavered, dark need brewing in her gaze. He inhaled, his lungs expanding at her blatant perusal. With a quick jerk, he tugged the buckle's peg from his belt and slid his hand over his hardened shaft bulging against his pants.

Her eyes widened.

Aramond chuckled. "You want this?"

Swollen and red from his kisses, she sucked her bottom lip into her mouth. A nod was all the confirmation he needed. She stretched on the bed, her taut nipples hard and begging for his touch.

He tugged on his fly, releasing the buttons with one quick thrust. The head of his shaft poked over the top of his underwear.

"Come here," she purred, scooting to the edge of the bed.

He toed off his boots and slid his jeans and underwear off in one fell swoop. Hot and heavy, his erection strained toward her, as if eager for her touch.

Danae didn't disappoint. After wrapping her fingers around his shaft, she squeezed. Lightning bolts of desire traveled to his balls and he almost came right then and there.

Out of pure instinct, he twisted his fingers in her hair, holding her in place. Danae stiffened, and he loosened his grip, rubbing his fingertips along her nape. The muscles in her shoulders relaxed, and the air he hadn't realized he'd held eased from his lips.

She tangled her fingers in the short hair around his balls, teasing him with her touch. A purr of pure admiration rumbled in her throat. Before Aramond could blink, she licked him from base to tip.

A tremor of need wracked his body. He'd never wanted a female like he wanted Danae.

She ran her tongue around the edge of his crown, her plump, reddened lips slipping over the tip.

His cat screamed inside, and a single word formed. *Mine.*

The rightness of it soaked beneath his skin, traveled along his nerves, and buried itself in his heart. He loved her, more than he should, but he wasn't worthy.

He couldn't take anymore. With a quickness born of his species, he pushed her back onto the bed and straddled her, caging her in his arms, one leg between her thighs. "Danae, I want you…like this."

Scraping her nails up his back, she left a trail of welts, sparking his desire.

His inner cat growled, a deep possessive snarl. He kissed her, claiming her with his mouth, afraid if he didn't, he'd bite her, bind her to him. His inner cat screamed for him to do exactly that, but he loved her and wouldn't go back on his promise.

She met him tooth and nail, giving as much as she got.

His erection, heavy and hot, lay against her thigh. He pressed closer, sliding toward her mound. She spread her legs and her citrus scent invaded his senses, sending him into a frenzy. He couldn't wait any longer. Deliberately, he eased into her, slow and steady, back and forth, inch by inch, allowing her time to adjust to his size.

When he was all the way in, he stilled.

Danae rocked against him, wiggling and pressing, driving him mad.

Aramond kissed her chin, her cheek, her forehead, marking her again and again with his scent, claiming her in any way he could, except the final, permanent way.

She moved her hips, and damn him, but he couldn't stop himself, matching her rhythm. Their pace increased with each stroke, faster and faster.

Her nails dug into his back and she quivered against him. She cried out, her orgasm taking her down the slow road of pleasure. Her release triggered his own, and he came inside her, filling her. Instinctually, his fangs descended, and he scraped them along her throat, giving her gentle kisses along the way.

She tensed beneath him, her body rigid. A scream of pure fear ripped from her throat. She pushed against him, fighting, battling, scratching.

He scrambled off her and fell on his ass onto the floor. His body heat rose as a swirl of confusion blanketed his brain. "What...what's wrong?"

Danae scrambled from the bed and grabbed the dagger lying on the bedside table. Even in the dim light penetrating under the curtains, the tip glistened. Lines formed around her eyes, pain and regret etched in her features. "You promised. How could you?"

Aramond blinked. What had he done? The turbulence in his mind swirled.

A muffled sob escaped Danae's lips. Her fingers tore to her neck.

There was no mark. He hadn't bitten her. Had he tried? He wracked his brain, but all he remembered were the gentle kisses. *...and my elongated fangs.* Although everything inside of him had screamed to claim her, he'd held back, honoring her request.

"I...I didn't—"

"That's because I didn't give you the chance. You lied to me. Get out!"

"That's not true. I wanted to bite you, yes, but..." He ran his hand over his face. How could he explain what was inside his heart without scaring her further? "I respect your decision. I wasn't going to—"

"I don't want to hear any more lies! You're nothing but trouble. Get out!" Her scream echoed off the ceiling, and her body shook with such force, he thought she'd fall over.

He glanced to the curtains. Sunlight. A lump formed in his stomach.

"There's a towel in the bathroom. Cover your head with it. Maybe you'll make it to the forest before you burn." Her words were like a stiff breeze, stoking the flames of her anger.

By the set of her jaw and the hard glint of determination in her eyes, this was not the time to argue with her. He'd come back later, try to explain himself better, tell her that he loved her. A dryness coated the back of his throat. Yes...he loved her, more than he could say.

"We need to talk about this when you have a clearer head. I'll return later." He picked up his clothes and boots from the floor.

"Don't. Just don't." Danae's voice wavered.

Aramond peered at her. Red-rimmed, her eyes gleamed with unshed tears. He'd caused that, and she'd kicked him out, just like he knew she would.

That didn't stop him from wanting to pull her into his arms, kiss her until she relented, show her how much he loved her.

She wiggled the dagger. "I mean it. Don't come back."

His heart shattered at her feet. He tightened his grip around his clothes and left.

CHAPTER 13

He almost bit me. Danae's entire body shook, her legs threatening to give out underneath her.

Aramond's footsteps receded down the hallway. The stair creaked, its familiar sound bringing on a wave of tears. She'd managed to hold back the flood gates in front of him, but now that he was gone, a sob escaped her lips.

Pressing her clenched fist against her mouth, she stifled a tormented scream. *I should've known it wouldn't work with a Taurus.*

She tossed the knife into the bedside table's drawer and slammed it shut. The lamp shimmied, and she gripped the shade before the thing tumbled to the ground. How could she have trusted him? He'd betrayed her just like Dradon, just like her father.

She tracked her trembling fingers to her scar. Aramond's teeth, one sharp, one jagged, had grazed across her neck. Goosebumps formed over her skin, and she prickled at the memory.

The fear had overwhelmed her, but if she was honest with herself, she had to admit there was a part of her that had wanted him to bite her.

That's what scared her more than anything. She'd wanted him to claim her as his mate.

I love him.

Deep inside, the rightness of those words rang in her heart. Then, why was she so afraid? *Because he'll control me, just like Dradon.*

He's not like that. She thought back to her time with him, before she'd turned fifteen and life became complicated. She'd only known him a few short months since he'd joined the Pride, but he'd always treated her with such respect. Her chest tightened, and a niggle of doubt crept inside.

He'd said he wasn't going to...what? Bite her? That's what he'd meant. Did he tell her the truth? She couldn't think, confusion stealing any attempt at conscious thought. Yet, an image crossed her mind...a vision of Aramond's red eyes. Filled with reverence, respect, and love, they were so different from Dradon's. She bit her lip, her breath catching in her throat.

I made a mistake and kicked him out, just like his mother.

The realization tore through her, shredding her insides. Her mind flitted to something he'd said last night. *Chantre, Aramie's mother...she kicked me out before her scent changed, saying I was too much trouble.* Seems he'd had a string of females tell him he was...too...much...trouble. Now, Danae had done the exact same thing.

She brought her fist to her mouth and sank her fangs into the soft flesh between her thumb and forefinger. Pain rippled up her arm, but the twinge was far less than the anguish tearing through her heart. After what she'd done to him, she deserved far worse.

She inhaled.

Maybe Aramond hadn't left, perhaps he was downstairs waiting for her. Hope, fragile and light, toyed with her nerves. She grabbed her pants and shirt, dressing with an urgent need. Wiping the tears from her eyes, she ran from her room, following his path down the stairs.

The creak echoed, pounding like a sledgehammer against her

psyche. Her foot slipped on the last step, but she righted herself, raced through the living room, and into the kitchen.

Half expecting to see him seated in one of the chairs, her gaze flicked to the table. All the seats were empty. The world spun and heaviness settled onto her shoulders. She leaned against the counter. Parched and dry, the ache in her throat only added to her torment.

Eager for a glass of water, she wrapped her fingers around the cupboard door and opened it. The movement sent a breeze over her cheeks, along with Aramond's scent.

She stilled.

The usual cry of the hinge was gone. Somewhere along the way, he'd oiled it, fixing the small annoyance because she'd complained about it, fixing it because he cared. A new bout of pain filtered into her heart. She let it fester, build, until the agony brought her to her knees. The bare wood, cold and hard, permeated through her jeans and into her skin, chilling her. A tear slid over her lash, tracking down her cheek. Another followed in its path.

She lay on the hardwood floor, the wood's rich smell chasing away Aramond's scent. The tears continued, her mind drifting over 'what ifs' and 'could've beens' until sleep, tormented as it was, finally claimed her.

～

Aramond swiped the towel over the back of his neck. A bird's solitary song flitted by on a breeze, answered by its mate. He crouched farther into the small hollow between the fallen tree and the hillside. The branches and the dense foliage provided enough coverage from the sun, but an occasional ray penetrated through the thick leaves. He rubbed the blister covering the back of his hand.

Propelled by pain and disappointment, he'd run far into the forest, now and then bits of filtered sunshine scorching his skin.

As soon as it was dark, he'd return, try to convince Danae that he wouldn't bite her, or not at least, without her permission.

Ah hell, who was he kidding?

She'd made it very clear she didn't want him around, kicking his sorry ass out of there, just like the others. Gee, what a surprise... Yet, he'd hoped things were different with Danae. He loved her, and he thought she cared for him as well, but maybe that was what he'd wanted to believe.

The sun painted the clouds in shades of pink and purple, indicating the end of the day. Soon, he could move from his self-imposed hell hole. Should he return to her? Was he a glutton for punishment? Apparently so.

He ground his teeth. No matter what, he'd tell her what was in his heart and let the aftermath dictate their future. Tension squeezed the muscles in his back, tightening them to the point of pain. *Lamont.*

The rogue Panthera was still on the prowl. At some point, he'd return, try to claim Danae for his own. Aramond's inner cat screamed in protest, the sound ripping from his throat and bouncing off the trees.

The birds' sweet calls silenced. The entire forest stilled.

His growl reverberated low in his chest. Claws emerged from his fingertips. *No, absolutely not.*

The primal need to protect *his* female spun through him. A thin film coated his eyes, coloring his world in shades of crimson. *I will hunt down this male and chase him from my territory.* The vow wound around his heart, securing itself into his soul.

He would protect Danae with his life.

CHAPTER 14

The moment the sun's last ray slipped behind the horizon, a ping resounded in Aramond's chest. His Panthera blood picked up the shift, the change from day to night. He pushed his palm against the fallen cedar, the rough bark abrading his skin. Emerging from his hiding place, he scanned the darkening sky.

Between the trees, a few scattered stars twinkled, growing brighter with each second. The faint outline of Orion's belt glimmered and in it, Lemuria...home.

Without hesitation, he slipped into his panther form. The scents of the forest—pine, wet foliage, deer—filtered into his senses. A low snarl, dark and predatory, erupted from his lips, turning into a loud growl. His panther wanted to pursue the buck, the desire to chase burning through his veins, but he reined in his inner cat.

He had something much more important on his mind. Danae.

A sense of urgency slid over his fur. Lamont would return soon. Adrenaline surged through Aramond's veins, and he bolted through the trees. As he ran, his nails dug into the soft loam, kicking dirt into the air.

The dire need to return to Danae sent a burst of energy to his muscles, propelling him onward. He relished the chance to beat his rival, chase him away, banish him from Aramond's territory. *Yes, mine.*

In so many ways, he'd claimed the area around Danae's home. His lungs expanded, the rightness of it melding into his soul. Even if she refused him, nothing would stop him from protecting her.

Heavy breaths eased in and out of his lungs. A scent he recognized, the sweet fragrance of strawberries, caught him off-guard. He slowed, coming to rest beside a large boulder in a small clearing. A female panther, her eyes slits of gold, emerged from behind a pine tree. *Aramie.*

Aramond's chest expanded. He shifted, returning to human form, his torn T-shirt and dark pants reforming over his skin.

His daughter transformed as well. Her dark shirt and leather pants matched her short black hair and deep brown eyes. The only bit of color, the strawberry barrette pinned in her shiny tresses. She ran toward him, her arms open, outstretched, welcoming.

When she reached him, he picked her up, twirling her around like he'd wanted to—if only he'd had the opportunity. Meeting as adults, he'd never had the chance to watch her grow up. She'd turned out to be a beautiful, strong female.

His lungs expanded, filling his chest with her sweet scent.

He placed her on the ground and trailed a finger over her chin. "What are you doing here?"

She smiled and leaned into his palm. "Hunting for Gossum. Rumor has it there's been an increase in activity in this area. We came to investigate."

"We?" Movement over her shoulder caught his attention. He flared his nostrils, scenting the air, but whoever was there was downwind. He could guess though. "Demir."

"Hello, Aramond." The Panthera leader stepped from the

shadows into the clearing. Dressed in dark pants and a black shirt, he was tall and muscular. With his hair tied back in a short queue, his face looked rugged. The moonlight glinted off the diamond stud in his nose.

Aramond's hackles rose, the lone alpha in him unwilling to bow to another male, but this was Aramie's mate and he'd come to terms with Demir. He gave the Pride leader a quick nod in greeting, his gaze never leaving Demir's. "It's good to see you again."

Demir stepped next to Aramie and put his arm around her shoulder. He raised an eyebrow. "Didn't expect to find you here. What can you tell us about the Gossum?"

His eyelid twitched, the skin jerking as if it had a mind of its own. He didn't have time for this. Instead, he needed to move, return to Danae's place before Lamont arrived, but he wouldn't disrespect Demir or Aramie. "I ran into one a couple of nights ago. It was a bit odd, actually." He ran his hand through his hair. "The creature wanted to bargain with me. Said there was an influx of troops arriving from the north, and wanted to know if I'd join them. Flip sides in the war."

A low growl eased from Demir, deep and powerful. "Impossible. That can't happen."

Aramond scowled. He clamped his teeth together, biting his tongue. The tang of blood filled his mouth. "I don't lie."

Aramie stepped between them, placing her palm on his chest. "No one said you did."

He let out a breath. "Forgive me. There's a male, Lamont. He's after my...female." The word tumbled from his mouth, odd and strange, but the rightness of it rang true to his ears. "I must intercept him before he claims her."

Demir nodded and tensed. "Understandable."

Aramie inhaled, her eyes narrowing.

The astringent scent of Gossum, more than one, burned the inside of Aramond's nose. The smell came from the direction of

Danae's house. Aramond's gut tightened around a firm ball of fear. She was alone.

"Follow me." He shifted and bolted before either Demir or Aramie could respond.

Their growls and their nails clicking against the bark and twigs indicated they weren't far behind. He ran faster than he thought possible, dread's cold fingers tingling his spine.

CHAPTER 15

*D*anae's foot tingled, sharp jabs waking up her numb appendage. She rubbed her aching skin, forcing blood to circulate. Still on the kitchen floor, a long sigh eased from her lips. How long had she stayed here?

Through the windows above the table, darkness claimed the cloudless sky. Stars forming the outline of Orion twinkled along the horizon, his arrow forever aimed at Taurus who seemed to charge toward him. She drew on the strength of the constellations and hauled herself to a standing position.

The tick, tick, tick of the kitty clock grew louder with each ping. Seven thirty-two, the stray hands indicated. What night is it? She forced herself to focus, her fingers trailing over her twin scars. *Tuesday.* Her shoulders relaxed. At least she didn't have any appointments tonight. She was in no shape for a palm or tarot card reading.

Where was Aramond? Would he return? He'd said as much, but doubt, lonely and headstrong crept inside her heart. She stepped past the table, noting the romance books holding up one end. Her fingers traced over one of the spines. So much for her happily ever after. She shook her head and tugged at the edge of the curtain.

The sliver of a new moon provided only a minimum amount of light, but it was enough for her Panthera eyes. Her gaze darted over the lawn to the wood pile, where a stack of new kindling leaned against the shed.

Aramond had cut that wood for her.

Biting her lip, she forced herself not to cry, not again. She traced the edge of the forest, searching for any sign, something that indicated he'd returned. All was still, quiet. She released the curtain, letting the soft material fall back into place.

What now? Good question.

She raised her chin. Since Dradon's death, she'd survived on her own. She'd do so again. Time to move on. Yet, her feet seemed rooted in place, her heart unwilling to cooperate with her mind. Her vision blurred, tears threatening again. She blinked them away and with determined strides, she headed for the living room.

A rapping at the back door. She stilled.

Hope, fragile and weak, flared to life in her chest. Aramond?

With the speed of her panther, she ran to the back door. In such a hurry, she'd forgotten that Aramond had covered the broken windows with plywood. She couldn't see who was on the other side, but...it had to be him. Her heart still light with hope, she gripped the handle and tugged.

The door swung open, creating a slight breeze and bringing the scent of fire embers and coal. Her senses registered the danger just as her eyes locked onto Lamont.

Her veins filled with something cold and hard.

She took a step back and reached for her dagger. Her fingers closed around nothing. She'd spent the day asleep on the floor, her weapon still in the bedside table's drawer.

"Hello, Danae." He grabbed her forearm, his grip so hard pain lanced all the way to her shoulder.

She yanked against his hold. "Let me go. You aren't welcome here."

"I will be, as soon as you are my mate." He smiled, baring his fangs. His free hand wrapped around her other arm and he dragged her through the door.

Her nails elongated. She tried to scratch him, but his grip was so tight, she couldn't get any leverage, couldn't reach him.

He hauled her down the two steps, and she stumbled, almost running into him. Before he could grab her, she shifted, turning into her panther. No way was she going to make this easy for him. If she didn't have her dagger, she'd use her natural weapons —her teeth and claws.

Unable to contain her in his human form, he released her. She backed up, putting as much space between them as possible. The thought to run whipped through her, but she'd never outrun him.

He'd take her down from behind, making it easier to bite her.

That she couldn't allow.

He shifted, his long, sleek coat glistening in the faint moonlight and stalked toward her, the muscles in his shoulders rippling. He raised his hackles, baring his fangs. His eyes were scarlet, the determined, evil intent bringing back the memory of Dradon and that fateful night so long ago.

She growled a warning, baring her fangs in response.

The muscles in his back legs bunched. He launched himself in mid-air. Energy surged through her and she met him half-way, his powerful chest slamming into her. A whoosh of air exploded from her lungs. Unable to breathe, agony rippled through her.

She scraped her paw down his back. His weight overpowered her and they crashed to the ground. The soft grass cushioned their fall, but her ribs screamed from the impact. At last, she inhaled. Cool air filtered into her lungs.

His larger body pinned her beneath him. Lamont's breath, warm and putrid, cascaded over her cheek.

She snarled and lashed out with her claws, but couldn't get

any purchase, his weight holding her down. He tried to bite her throat, but she moved her head, blocking him with her face. His fang scraped along her cheek.

With a determined growl, she bit him on the nose. He growled and slapped his paw across her face. The stars in the sky appeared to dance. Taurus's red eye mocked her, his visage laughing. She blinked, clearing her head in time to see the white tips of Lamont's fangs descending toward her throat.

CHAPTER 16

*A*ramond bounded between the trees, his paws scraping through the dirt, digging into the moist soil. The astringent smell of Gossum intensified, wreaking havoc with Aramond's senses. Programmed into his very soul was the urgent need to fight his enemy. The powerful force burned, hot and fast through his veins, spurring him onward.

In the distance, a faint light glowed through the windows of Danae's home. Closer now, the Gossum's bitter tang coated the back of his throat. Yet underneath the stench was another distinct smell, the dark, smoky aroma of embers and coal —Lamont.

Aramond's blood roared in his ears. A fresh burst of adrenaline rushed through him, fueled by his unstoppable need to protect Danae.

He broke through the trees into her back yard. Like skates on ice, his paws slid over the moist dew coating the grass. A small squeak emanated from the broken blades. His attention riveted on two figures at the foot of the outside porch stairs. A larger cat pinned a smaller one to the ground—Lamont and Danae.

His heart skipped a beat. Was he too late? *No, not again.*

Near the shed, a line of Gossum emerged from the shadows. Awareness of Demir and Aramie behind him flitted over his senses.

Let them handle the enemy. He had his own opponent to fight. Aramond snarled and bolted toward the house.

Danae bit Lamont on the nose. The male snarled and scraped his paw over Danae's face. Her head whipped to the side.

A sheen of red descended over Aramond's vision. He closed the distance.

Danae blinked, but her unfocused gaze was on the stars.

A Gossum ran across the lawn toward Aramond. Its long knife-like nails gleamed in the light. He'd have to fight the beast before he could reach Danae. His jaw tightened to the point of pain.

He veered toward his natural enemy. At the quick turn, his paw lost purchase on the wet grass. His leg slid out from underneath him. Fast and hard, his hindquarter hit the ground. His gaze veered to Danae.

Lamont opened his jaw and bared his fangs. He lowered his head, aiming his bite for her shoulder.

No! Bile rose in Aramond's throat. He stood, the muscles in his legs rigid.

The Gossum snapped its tongue, just missing Aramond's ear. Spittle landed on his face.

Aramond scraped his claws down the creature's arm, digging deep into the flesh. A scream rent from the beast. The end of its barbed tongue connected with Aramond's shoulder.

Pain crept under his skin, but adrenaline fueled by his anger kept the numbing effect at bay. With a burst of energy, Aramond scraped his claws over the Gossum's throat. The creature stilled, his body tense for a moment before relaxing into a pile of black sludge. With a quick jerk, Aramond turned around.

Danae.

~

Trapped beneath Lamont, Danae couldn't move. Her attention drew to his mouth. A drop of spittle hung on the end of one canine, gleaming in the light. Dread's cold fingers travelled up her spine.

She bucked against him, trying in vain to escape his hold, but his big body had her pinned. *Fight, fight!* Before she could question her choice, she transformed into her human form. His weight almost crushed her, and she couldn't breathe.

The abrupt change must've startled him for he hesitated. The saliva on his fang dripped onto her face. White spots formed in her vision. If she didn't get a breath soon, she'd pass out. Using what little strength she had left, she tugged on her hand, freeing it from between their bodies. With a quick thrust, she poked him in the eyes.

A feral cry rang into the night. His hold on her loosened. She dragged in air, gulping with eager anticipation.

A flash of black rushed toward them. In the next instant, Lamont's weight lifted from her. Snarls and growls erupted in the air.

Aramond! She scooted back, out of the way.

The two males fought in the grass. Aramond was bigger, and soon he had Lamont pinned. A low growl rumbled from Aramond. He demanded the other male submit to him, his jaw clamped around Lamont's throat.

Her mouth went dry as relief cascaded over her shoulders. She took a large breath. The bitter tang of Gossum raced down her throat. So focused on Lamont, she hadn't noticed the astringent smell. Movement on the other side of the lawn caught her attention. Four Gossum fought two Panthera. Who were they?

One of the Gossum broke away from the other Panthera, heading toward them. "Aramond. Watch out."

His gaze focused on her then turned toward the bigger threat —the Gossum.

Lamont used the distraction to his advantage. He bucked against Aramond, managing to escape his grip. He scrambled several feet away. His red eyes focused on her, and his lip curled over his fang. He turned away, slinking toward the forest.

Aramond took a step toward her, using his body as a shield, protecting her. Even under the dire circumstances, Danae's chest expanded. *He loves me.*

The Gossum chuffed and came to a stop several feet away. His gaze wandered to Lamont. "Where do you think you're going?" he hissed.

The muscles in Lamont's back and hindquarters visibly stiffened under his fur. He turned his attention to the Gossum. Snarling, he transformed into his human form. "I plan to live to fight another day."

"You said there would be only one Panthera. You lied." The Gossum's eyes narrowed.

Lamont shrugged. "You outnumbered them. Not my fault they beat you."

The Gossum glanced over his shoulder. Only one of his companions remained. The other two Panthera now tackled their last enemy.

Aramond returned to his human form and retrieved a throwing star from his belt. He drew Danae to him, pulling her against his side. Her pulse raced, as much from the contact as the tenseness of the situation.

The creature's attention returned to Lamont. He took a step forward. "You set us up. You're a traitor's traitor."

Before Lamont could respond, the Gossum launched himself, claws outstretched. His tongue connected with Lamont's shoulder. Lamont screamed and morphed into his cat.

Aramond tugged on Danae's arm, dragging her away from the

skirmish. "C'mon. Let the creature have its revenge." She followed, eager to put some distance between them.

The fight didn't last long. A quick slice of a claw across Lamont's throat and he slid to the ground, a pile of sand was all that remained.

The Gossum turned to face her and Aramond. A tingle of fear traveled down her arms.

With a quick flick of Aramond's wrist, something small and quick flashed through the air. A soft thunk. The Gossum stilled, a throwing star embedded in one dark orb. It disintegrated into a pile of black goo.

"Are you okay?" Aramond's strained voice displayed his concern.

She touched her scar. So close... Her throat tightened. Aramond had saved her. She peered into his eyes. "Y...yes, thanks to you."

The lines around his beautiful eyes relaxed, and he drew her into his embrace. She snuggled against him, soaking up his strength, his scent, his love. *I belong here, in his arms.* The realization bloomed in her chest, feeling so right. Tears pinpricked her eyes.

"Who do we have here?" A male's deep voice carried along the breeze.

She stiffened and pulled back enough to glance at him.

He had brown eyes, a diamond stud in his nose, and dark hair tugged back in a queue. His presence had an air of authority.

Alpha male.

Was this Demir, the leader of the Pride that lived in the underground Keep?

Danae struggled to breathe. He'd force her to return with him and mate her off to a male.

CHAPTER 17

a slight breeze whipped through the trees at the edge of Danae's property, causing shadows to dance over her lawn, eerily reminiscent of sharp, pointed fangs. Goosebumps formed, tingling her skin.

Aramond tugged Danae tighter against him, and his strength eased around her like a warm blanket. She appreciated his desire to protect her, but she wanted to stand up to Demir on her own, damn the consequences. There was no way she'd let him force her to bond to a male. *Not unless it was Aramond.*

The stray thought wound into her chest, filtering into her heart. She longed to be Aramond's mate, but she wanted to make the choice, not have it forced upon her.

Demir cleared his throat. He'd asked who she was, a question neither she nor Aramond had answered.

She bit her lip, trying not to let her fear show.

A female with short dark hair and a red barrette strode up next to Demir. She placed her hand on his shoulder. "Demir, you're scaring her."

He exhaled and wrapped his fingers over the female's. "Not my intent."

She smiled and touched Danae's arm. Her fingers were soft, gentle. "I'm Aramie. Please excuse my mate. He can be a bit over-bearing at times."

Danae's gaze flicked to Aramie's throat and the twin scars that marred her skin. "He's your mate?"

Aramie had spoken so brazenly about him, yet, the love for him was evident in her eyes. Could Danae be wrong about Demir?

Aramie chuckled. "Yes, he's our Pride leader, but once in a while he forgets his manners, and I'm the only one that's allowed to rein him in."

Demir wrapped his hand around Aramie's waist and planted a tender kiss on her head. "Just so we're clear, no one else has that privilege."

Danae glanced from Aramond to Aramie. The likeness in their dark hair and strong features was unmistakable. She peered at Aramond. "Aramie, she's the daughter you mentioned."

He glanced at Aramie, and a smile bloomed on his face. "Yes, she's my daughter. Demir, Aramie, this is Danae, my..." He clamped his mouth shut. A tic started in his jaw.

Danae wrapped her fingers around his and gave him a gentle squeeze. "We have a long history. Knew each other before..." Her fingers traced to her scar.

Demir cleared his throat. "If you've lost your mate, you are welcome to return to the Keep with us. I'm sure there's plenty of males that would love to court you."

Her throat tightened. She didn't want anyone else but Aramond, but she wouldn't say that, not here, not in front of them. Instead, she blurted, "You won't force me to mate to one of them?"

Aramond's entire body tensed. He drew in an audible breath.

Demir's gaze flitted from her to Aramond and back again. A slow smile tugged at his lips. "Not at all. Aramie cured me of my errant, backward ways. You are free to choose a male, if that's what you want."

The tension in her shoulders eased, but she didn't want to go with them. Instead, she wanted to stay here with Aramond and run her safe house. That wouldn't work though, he was a rogue warrior, his job was to track and kill the stray Gossum. Her chest ached, and she glanced at her home.

Aramie turned her attention to the house. "Do you live here?"

"I do." She bit her lip.

"For how long?" Aramie asked.

The soft reassurance in her voice broke through Danae's walls. "A few months. I set up a safe house for the rogue Panthera warriors. They come here for medical attention, a free meal, and a place to stay for the day. I run a palm and tarot card reading for the human locals and tourists to earn money. It's been wonderful to—"

Demir raised his hand.

Danae held her breath. Did he disapprove? What would she do if he forced her to quit, made her go with them to the Keep?

Aramond rubbed his hand down her arm, comforting her and taking away some of the chill. She leaned against him, thankful for his support.

"There are many rogue alpha males around," Demir's gaze darted to Aramond, "that won't join us in the Keep." His focus returned to Danae. "I support your efforts to assist in this war, but…"

Here it was, his rejection. Danae held her breath.

"I think you could use some additional security around here. I'd like to assign one of my warriors to watch over you, unless," his gaze tracked to Aramond, "you have someone in mind for the job."

A lightness lifted her spirit. She turned to face Aramond. "Aramond, would you stay here with me? Help me run this place?"

He trailed a finger through her hair and wiped away a stray strand that had caught in her eyelash. His tender gesture burrowed into her heart, but there was something amiss in his furrowed brow.

"As much as I want to stay here with you, I can't. The thought of male after male traipsing through here. It would drive me insane unless you were my…" He pursed his lips.

Mate. That was the unspoken word. Warm and hot, her pulse spiked, and unable to stop it, she secreted some of her pheromones. The scent of citrus filled the air.

The muscles in his chest and arms tightened beneath his white shirt. "Don't tease me, Danae."

"So long ago, I'd dreamed of becoming your mate. Over these past few days, you've reminded me what love is. You helped me get over my fear."

"What are you saying?"

Her chest expanded as her decision solidified. "Aramond, I would love to be your mate, if you'll have me."

He pulled her to him, wrapping his strong arm around her waist while his free hand cupped her cheek in his palm. His breath, warm and enticing, tickled her skin. "Over the many years of my life I've only wanted you, but are you sure this is what you want?"

She nodded. "Yes, I'm sure."

He bared his fangs, one sharp, the other jagged, and his eyes turned crimson.

She'd never seen anything so sexy. Tilting her head, she stretched her neck, giving him maximum exposure. "Whenever you're ready, Aramond."

A sharp pin-prick of pain blossomed as his teeth sank into the soft spot between her shoulder and throat. Heat radiated through her chest.

I'm a mated female.

He withdrew his fangs and licked the wound. With a tenderness she'd grown to love, he kissed her, claiming her again, showing her through his actions how much he loved her. She relished in his affection, her love for him bringing forth a round of tears.

He broke their kiss and held her head between his palms. Lines formed around his eyes, fear embedded deep in their depths. "You're crying. What—"

"Sh...sh..." She ran her fingers over his lips. "These are tears of joy."

The tension in his arms released, and he brought her head to his chest. His unique scent enveloped her as he rubbed his nimble fingers at the base of her neck. "My Danae."

"Well. Congratulations, you two." Demir chuckled.

Danae peered at the Pride leader. He beamed with his approval.

Aramie smiled and stepped forward, her arms outstretched. "Danae, I'm so glad to have you as part of the family."

Aramond tugged his daughter into their joint hug. Danae's chest expanded, a happiness she hadn't known filling her on the inside. She wanted to stay this way, but it wasn't long before Aramond released them.

Danae placed her fingers on Aramie's arm. "Would you two like to come in for a few minutes? There are some cookies inside. I'd love the chance to get to know my new family." Her throat squeezed the words, bottling them up.

Demir stepped forward and placed his hand on Aramond's shoulder. "That would be nice. I've wanted some time to get to know my father-in-law, but I think we'll save that for next time."

"Yes, we should go, give the new couple some private time." She winked. "We'll be back though. Demir can't resist cookies, and I do want to chat."

Demir tugged at Aramie's waist, leading her toward the forest. In a few moments, they were gone.

Aramond wrapped his hand around Danae's waist. "Did you say you have cookies?" His wicked smile made her pulse race.

She giggled. "Oh, you get the house special, my love. A batch only for you."

He swiped his hands beneath her knees, scooping her up, and cradled her against him. With determined strides, he headed for the back door. A soft chuckle eased from him. "As you wish, my love, as you wish."

CHAPTER 18

*D*anae crouched behind a cedar tree, the pads of her feet resting against a fern's soft fronds. The plant's curling tip tickled her nose, toying with her whiskers. She waited, biding her time. Sniffing the air, she searched for Aramond's scent, the one forever etched in her mind and her heart.

The wind shifted, and his unique scent of earth and fresh rain carried along the breeze.

She burst from her hiding spot, running over the ferns and small plants growing between the tall cedars and pines. A low growl caught her attention.

He was close.

Her skin tingled as awareness of him settled over her nerves. A heady rush of desire flooded her bloodstream. She ran on, faster, but it was only a matter of time before he took her down.

Brush rustled. A twig snapped.

She jumped over a downed log. A paw, claws contracted, slid over her haunch. She shivered with delight. Up ahead, her destination—the ravine. If she could make it there before he tackled her, she'd win this game of theirs.

Hope flitted along her nerves, whether it was for her to

succeed or for him to catch her first, she wasn't quite sure. Both had advantages.

She slid past an uprooted tree that leaned against its neighbor, roots pointing in all different directions like a hand with many fingers. The momentary observation cost her the advantage. In the next instant, she was pressed into wet ferns, her muzzle buried in Aramond's soft fur. For the briefest moment, his weight pinned her to the ground, but he rolled, bringing her to rest alongside him. He nuzzled the back of her ear, a purr rumbling in his chest.

She transformed into her human state and turned to face him.

His eyes gleamed a vibrant shade of red, passion and love for her radiating in their depths. She stroked his whiskers and ran her fingers over his thick fur coat, relishing in everything that was Aramond...her mate.

Joining her in human form, he pulled her to him for a bruising kiss. His lips lingered on hers, revealing in so many ways how much he cared for her, loved her. She melded into him, enjoying the moment and his affectionate attention. He broke the kiss, and their combined panting echoed between them.

Her mate reached under her arm and tickled her ribs. She batted away his hand, stood and glanced past the ravine's edge. The new moon was a shadow against the sky. Stars from faraway galaxies twinkled and winked.

"The stars are calling your name." She cupped her hand over her ear. "Aramond... Aramond..."

He rose, his massive height dwarfing her in his shadow. His chuckle reverberated off the trees.

With forced surprise, she placed her fingers over her mouth. "Don't you hear them?"

"Indeed. But I think they call your name." He glanced around the small clearing at the edge of the ravine. A large pine tree stood nearby, some of its branches leaning over the brink.

Slowly, a smile tugged at his lips. "This is where we ran into each other. Hard to believe that was only a short month ago."

She leaned into him, her breasts pressing against his rock hard muscles. With a moan of pure feminine appreciation, she brushed her lips against his. He kissed her, his mouth eager and hungry, reminding her, once again, why she'd agreed to mate with him.

An owl hooted then launched itself into the air from a nearby tree. It circled over the ravine as if it didn't have a care in the world.

Danae tugged on Aramond's hand, pulling him toward her favorite tree. She slid her hands around his waist, and he wrapped her in his warm embrace. This is what she'd always wanted, mated to a male who respected her and loved her. Amelia was right. Maybe the older woman should do her own tarot card readings. Danae couldn't wait for her to meet Aramond.

She glanced at the owl, but her gaze was soon drawn to the stars. Without conscious thought, she sought out Orion, his belt, and Lemuria, her home. As she'd done so many times before, her focus shifted to the 'V' in the Taurus constellation and Aldebaran, the red-orange star that colored the bull's eye.

She pointed to the grouping of stars. "Do you see Taurus?"

He followed her line of sight. "I see him. He's my zodiac sign, remember?"

With a gentle touch, she trailed a finger over his cheek. "Yes, I know. I used to hate him and his red eye, full of possessive anger."

"Really?" He cocked his brow and drew her tight against him. His erection pressed into her abdomen, hot and hard. For the briefest moment, his eyes flared red. "Used to?"

She shimmied against him, teasing him with the material separating them. "Now, all I see is you and your eyes that gleam red with your passion and love."

He purred, the low sound rumbling in his chest. Pressed

against him, her nipples tightened at the vibration and at the promise of something more. "That's good. Taurus, and those under his sign, are very sensual and passionate. Shall I remind you?"

Her body responded, sending a rush of desire to her core. The scent of lemons filled the air.

"I'll take that as a yes." He cradled her head in his palm. With deliberate tenderness, he trailed kisses down her throat until he came to her scars, the one's he'd created. He licked them, circling his tongue over the marks. "My mate, my love."

"Yes, my mate, my love. Always yes." The words tumbled from her lips, and her heart expanded so much her chest ached. Mated and in the arms of the male she loved, she couldn't be happier.

$\sim$

Enjoyed reading Aramond and Danae's story? Want to read more about the Panthera? Delve into the war over Earth's most precious resource—water—and the fate of humankind in the *Warriors of Lemuria* series. Turn the page for a sneak peek at book 1, ***Untouchable Lover***.

SNEAK PEEK - UNTOUCHABLE LOVER

BOOK 1 IN THE WARRIORS OF LEMURIA SERIES

CHAPTER 1

Stale air and mildew assailed Melissa's nose. She tried to swallow, but the thick smell coated her throat. Lifting her head, she opened her eyes. Light blinded her, sending a sharp jolt of pain through her skull. *Where am I?*

She stood erect, her backside pressed against a solid, cold surface. Dampness coated her skin. A thin line of drool spilled from her mouth and onto her chin. She raised her hand to wipe the wetness away, only to discover chains bound her wrists. The iron manacles rattled, echoing off the cement walls. A drop of fear weaseled its way into her mind. She inhaled, and a wave of dizziness passed over her.

The pungent smell of rubbing alcohol filtered into the cell, the telltale sign of Gossum. Melissa's throat constricted, and she gagged. She'd never get used to that stench, not as long as she lived. She winced. That might not be for much longer.

Memories of the Gossum attack raised her pulse and made her shiver. She didn't want to think about why this had happened, why she'd left the safety of her Pride, but she couldn't stop herself. Her heart clenched, and she choked back a sob.

She'd left Denver in search of another Pride, one where maybe, just maybe, she'd be accepted for who she was and not ridiculed for being different. As the only Dren in recent memory to conceive and birth a child, the rest of the Pride either hated her from petty jealousy or wanted to own her. She'd traveled as far as Portland, Oregon, before her need to feed drove her to seek a human male.

Luring a man out of a grocery store late at night, she couldn't bring herself to drink from him. He would've found the sensation pleasurable, and she wouldn't have taken enough blood to kill him, but the human frailty reflected in his eyes, and his likeness to William, her dead mate, had squashed any desire of feeding. She'd fled the scene as far as her feet would take her.

Her enemy found her as she'd stumbled into the warehouse district. Weak from her unwillingness to feed, she wasn't able to maintain her shield. They'd caught her between the old brick buildings. She shuddered at the recollection.

Denver seemed so far away. A ball of regret grew in her stomach. If she'd stayed, she'd be Demir's concubine by now. As ruler of the Pride, he'd wanted her to come to him on her own. When she hadn't, he'd become so enraged she'd feared for her life. What would become of her now? Despair lodged itself in her chest, festering, building until a layer of sweat coated her body.

"Don't fear. They can smell it," a masculine voice said. "They'll be back soon enough."

Across the room, a tall male stood shackled to the wall. Not only did he have arm and leg chains, but cuffs surrounded his neck and torso as well. One arm had a design etched into his skin that ended with four dark lines down the back of his hand. Intelligence shone from one pale blue eye. The other one was darkened with bruising and swollen shut. He looked like he'd seen more than his share of pain and heartache. Although his short brown hair didn't have any grey, the lines in his face indicated he wasn't young. Neither Gossum nor human, he was a species she'd never met.

"Who are you—and where are we?" she asked.

"I'm Gaetan. We're in the Gossum's care, so to speak." His voice was rough, strained.

"Why capture us? Why not just kill us?" The bastard Gossum killed her mate and young son the year before. Her mind fought the horrific images and memories, anything to stop her from going insane with grief. She bit the side of her mouth to stifle a wail of sorrow. Still, a soft whimper escaped.

"That is the question of the hour," he said.

Cuts and bruises marred his arms and legs. When he breathed, his breaths were shallow as if he were in great pain. His left leg was smaller than his right and misshapen, forcing him to lean to the left. They had tortured him. When would they come back to finish the job?

Footsteps approached from the hallway. She tensed, and her pulse pounded in tune with each step.

A Gossum's massive body filled the entrance to her cell. The light from the corridor illuminated him from behind, and his face was a mask of shadows. He snickered. The low sound chilled her arms.

The large male stepped into the chamber, and his features became visible in the dim light. His grim face accentuated his bulbous nose. The brim of his cap covered the back of his neck.

From prior experience with Gossum, she knew he wore the hat to hide his bald head and the beginning of the hard scales that ran down his back. Although once human, he no longer required his eyelids to protect his hard, lizard-like, black eyes. They reflected the light with an eerie shine.

"Ah, good, you're awake. Are you ready to chat?" His menacing voice rasped with venom.

Melissa clamped her lips tight. The steady drip of water nearby echoed against the bare walls. Her damp hair hung in her eyes, the bitterly cold strands clung to her cheeks and arms.

His face turned red at her silence, but he remained calm. He leaned against the wall and crossed his arms. His yellow and black high-tops stood out like a beacon. He could still pass as human, given the right clothing to cover his hairless body and neck scales.

"Ignoring me won't help your cause," he said.

"Don't give in to his demands." Gaetan pulled against his chains.

Their jailer sauntered over to Gaetan. "Still with us, I see." He touched Gaetan's face, raking a claw over his cheek.

Gaetan snarled, and his good eye glowed with specks of gold.

"Oh, yeah, we're making progress." The vile creature chuckled. He turned toward Melissa, and a chilling smile revealed his serrated teeth, the ones he hid from the humans.

She shivered at the sight. Her life couldn't end this way, at the hands of her enemy. Memories of Seth and William raced through her mind, and a knot of determination formed in her stomach. She would fight for them, to honor their memory.

She yanked on her chains but only succeeded in opening cuts on her wrists. Blood trickled over her arm and dripped onto the concrete floor. She wanted to scream her rage at the Gossum, but she held her anger in check, barely.

Like a black cloud, their captor's presence filled the room. Even in his nonchalance his gaze pierced her, held her in place, while a cool bead of sweat rolled down the back of her neck. She feared him, but she wouldn't give her tormentor the satisfaction of seeing her weakness.

"Tell me your name, my dear." His soft and encouraging voice belied his evil intent.

She refused to speak, and instead, raised her chin.

"C'mon now, how is telling me your name going to hurt?" The corner of his mouth pulled into a smile. He returned to Gaetan and pointed, a claw extending like a crooked tree branch from his bony finger near the prisoner's good eye. "I like the sound of his howl. Would you like to hear it?"

Heat flushed through her body. Hatred burned in her gut for what they'd done to Gaetan. She wouldn't be the cause of more pain.

"Melissa," she spat. "My name is Melissa."

"Ah, much better. My name is Ram. Now we are acquainted." Ram placed his index finger next to his mouth and looked at the ceiling. "So, Melissa, about that shield of yours. I could do so much with it."

Melissa flinched at the mention of her gift. She tried to power her energy, but there wasn't even a spark. She held Ram's gaze and struggled to control her shaking knees.

"It's too bad I need you alive to get your blood. Lemurians disintegrate so quickly once dead that I can't get it fast enough." Ram tsked. "So, I'll give you a chance to cooperate."

"I won't give my shield to you." Melissa curled her hands into fists. He wanted her magical power, but no way would she give her special skill to the enemy.

Ram's smile turned into a grimace, and his easygoing demeanor evaporated. He became rigid, his muscles bunching in his arms and legs. His elongated tongue whipped in and out of his mouth, the dangerous spur at the tip coming close to her face.

She recoiled, and her head struck the hard cement wall. Stars swam in her vision, but she refused to succumb to the darkness. Dread snaked its way into her heart.

"As you wish." Ram snapped his fingers.

One of his brood entered the room carrying a cast iron

bucket. The top of a branding iron extended over the lip. A towel wrapped around the end protected the handle from the heat within the kettle. The smell of smoldering coal joined with the odors of sweat and fear.

Melissa's pulse quickened. She swallowed, but nothing went down. Her throat was too parched.

Ram grabbed the branding iron.

Adrenaline rushed through her body. "Wh-what is that for?"

"It's your incentive."

"No, don't, not her. Take me." Gaetan's voice, weak and rough, carried across the room.

Melissa glanced at him. They'd just met, but his willingness to protect her spoke volumes about his character.

Ram snapped to attention. "Oh, I intend to get what I need from you, Stiyaha. That abnormal strength of yours will be mine, just not yet. I will take her gift first."

Ram turned his focus back to Melissa. "I want your shield, and I want it now."

He closed the distance, the branding iron's heat radiating in the space between them. Her legs shook, making the shackles at her ankles clank together like an eerie wind chime. Her fear ratcheted up another level, sending a shiver of terror over her shoulders. She hated him all the more.

"Are you willing to bargain? Or are you going to be stubborn?" Ram leaned in, and his breath reeked of liquor. "I know you're Lemurian, but you're not Stiyaha. You must not be from around here. Tell me what you are," he purred, as he drew the back of a finger down the side of her face.

She flinched at his touch, but she wouldn't let him intimidate her. Making eye contact with her enemy, she held her ground.

"If you lead me to others like you, I'll let you walk away, unscathed," he said.

She bared her fangs. "I would never sell out my kind. I will fight you every step of the way."

"Well, now, that's what I thought you'd say." His eyes gleamed with delight, and his mouth curved into a grin. "Let's play, shall we?"

For more information on *Untouchable Lover*, visit www.rosalieredd.com.

ALSO BY ROSALIE REDD

Books in the *Warriors of Lemuria* series:
Untouchable Lover - book #1
Untamable Lover - book #2
Unimaginable Lover - book #3
Undeniable Lover - book #4 - **Coming 2017**
Unforgettable Lover - novella
Alora's Love Potion - short story collection
Marked by Love - novella

Reviews

Enjoyed *Marked by Love*? The best gift you can give an author is an honest review. Please consider leaving a review on your favorite retailer to help spread the word and support an author.

Newsletter

Want access to free reads, special offers, and giveaways? Sign up here for my newsletter on my website and you'll receive a **free ebook**. Don't worry, your information won't be shared with anyone but my muse. You can visit me at my website at www.rosalieredd.com or contact me at Rosalie@rosalieredd.com. I love to receive email from readers!

ABOUT ROSALIE

After finishing a rewarding career in finance and accounting, it was time for award-winning author Rosalie Redd to put away the spreadsheets and take out the word processor. She pens paranormal, science fiction, and fantasy romance in her office cave located in Oregon, where rain is just another excuse to keep writing.